PREQUEL TO THE REBEL QUEEN

THE
ROYAL
ARRANGEMENT

BY
JEANA E. MANN

HENRY

*W*ith a smile meant to please, the masked hostess shoves open enormous double doors into New York City's most exclusive sex club, the Devil's Playground. The vaulted ceiling soars upward, giving the twentieth-century warehouse the illusion of a castle. Women in colorful gowns flit like butterflies beneath glittering chandeliers. Men in tuxedos carry cigars, sip brandy from crystal snifters, and discuss the stock market. Excitement swirls in the air.

"Are you enjoying your evening, sir?" she asks.

"Yes, thank you." Even though I'm wearing a mask, I wait for her to recognize me. I have reason to be cautious. I'm the Crown Prince of Androvia. The one who lives in a castle, the one with a different car for each day of the week, the one who dampens panties with a smile. My face graces hundreds of tabloids each year. Someday, my portrait will hang in the Hall of Kings next to seven generations of monarchs. If she knows who I am, she doesn't let on, and the tension leaves my shoulders. "This is my first visit. Do you have any recommendations?"

"Are you looking for a companion or are you here to observe?" The brilliance of her smile increases as she gazes up at me.

"Observation only." Although an anonymous fuck with one of these lovely women is tempting, I'm here to meet with Roman Menshikov, co-owner of this fine establishment.

"You're in luck. This is a special night. All twelve of our custom playrooms are booked and available for your viewing pleasure." She sweeps a hand toward the nearest exit. "Through those doors. Enjoy."

A crowd swarms around the two-way glass of the first observation window. At six foot four, I can see over everyone's heads and straight into the playroom. No expense has been spared to recreate the interior of a medieval dungeon. Stone walls and floors and crude wooden furniture provide the perfect backdrop for the fantasy. The crowd presses closer to see the couple inside. I press closer too. Never in my twenty-seven years have I seen anything this primal, so erotic—and believe me, I've seen a lot.

The woman twists away from her shackles, muscles taut with pleasure. Jesus, she's stunning. Perky, bouncing breasts. Pale pink nipples. A waterfall of luxurious auburn hair cascades over her pale skin. Like everyone else in this place, a masquerade mask hides her face. She turns her head to the side, biting into her full lower lip with even white teeth. Her companion spanks a hand on her ass. His fingers leave red marks on the firm white flesh. A dizzying rush of blood evacuates my head and hastens to my dick.

"Can I help you with that?" The petite brunette at my elbow nods toward the erection tenting my tuxedo pants. Her invitation yanks me out of the spell cast by the scene.

The whole point of this evening is to see and be seen. If I say yes, no one will care. On the sofa behind us, a man has his head buried beneath the hem of a voluptuous woman's evening gown, one hand on his cock and the other on her bared breast.

"Not tonight."

"Are you sure?" The brunette smiles up at me. Below her jeweled mask, full lips pout.

"Yes." My gaze flits over her shoulder to the dungeon window. Her prom queen beauty pales in comparison to the goddess chained to the wall.

"Too bad. Your loss." She smiles then disappears into the shadowy corners of the hallway.

The man next to me pushes closer to the observation window, transfixed by the exhibition of submission and dominance. "She's perfection," he mutters. I can't agree with him more.

The couple on display is oblivious to the spectators. The woman pulls against her restraints, begging for discipline. Discipline I could give her. The need to punish and dominate is a smoldering ember in my subconscious, a hunger that no amount of vanilla sex has ever been able to satiate. I imagine the redhead's groans of pleasure. Tiny whimpers of ecstasy escaping her pouty mouth. Her partner turns his head to the side, giving me a good view of his profile. Even with a disguise, I recognize the straight nose, square jaw, and perfect brown hair of my former college roommate. Wanker. I hate Nikolay Reznik, also known as Nicky Tarnovsky, for a hundred reasons. First, because he's got something I want—this gorgeous redhead. And second, because the last time I saw him, he was balls deep in my fiancée.

3

EVERLY

Reeking of sex and shame and more exhilarated than I've been since my divorce, I wait for Nicky in the hallway. Nicky with his gray bedroom eyes, his hint of a Russian accent, and his large cock. The last place I ever intended to be was at a New York City sex club. Until he asked me. Until he whispered in my ear like Satan himself.

It's been at least thirty minutes since he left me in the dungeon room to deal with a work emergency. More than enough time for him to reach his office and come back for me. I sigh and dig through my clutch for a compact mirror to recheck my lipstick. That's the problem with dating one of the club owners. Business is always on the agenda. Although his absence is annoying, the extra minutes give me a chance to pull my head together. Minutes I need to clear the confusion caused by my first Devil's Playground experience.

"Pretty dress," a woman remarks as she passes by on the arm of a masked gentleman. The tail feathers of her mask jerk with each of her steps. She tilts her head toward her companion. "Isn't she lovely, darling?"

"Yes. Exquisite," her companion replies. He nods his head in acknowledgment. Like all the male guests, he wears a black tuxedo and mask.

"Thank you." Heat crawls along my skin. Do they know what I just did in the room behind me? Did they watch? I've never been secretive about my sex life. In my opinion, it's a natural and necessary part of life, one to be celebrated. The Devil's Playground, however, is way outside the normal limits of my comfort zone. It's a venue built for fantasies, the perfect place to escape the ugly reality of my life. Behind a mask and the protection of the club's twenty-six-page NDA, I can be anyone I like. No paparazzi. No judgment. No names or faces.

I want to blame my uncharacteristic wildness on a string of disheartening events. A husband who loved his administrative assistant more than me. The revelation that he fathered a child with this woman during our marriage. His betrayal chipped away at my self-esteem until I no longer know who I am or what I stand for. Months after our separation and divorce, I still feel the cracks in my confidence.

"Can I get you anything, madam?" Achilles, one of the club hosts, pauses at my side. He's the only person here, aside from my date, who knows my identity.

"No, thank you. I'm just waiting for my friend. He said to stay here, but he's been gone forever. Have you seen him?" I'm careful to avoid using names, one of the numerous house rules.

"He's been detained by a—customer." The hesitation in his statement sends a chill of foreboding through my body. "Perhaps you'd be more comfortable in one of the lounges or the bar? I can have him meet you there."

"That's okay. I'll be fine."

"I insist." He sweeps a hand to the left, encouraging me down the corridor in an unfamiliar direction. When I hesitate, his pleasant demeanor falters. "Please, madam. We need to clear this playroom for the next occupants. I'll have a complimentary bottle of champagne brought to you for the inconvenience, and I'll notify your date of your whereabouts."

"Alright." I turn in the direction of the large reception area, the same route Nicky used to bring me here.

"Not that way." Achilles steps in front of me. "The other way."

An ill foreboding snakes down my body. This isn't the way I came in. Then again, maybe I'm being rerouted to protect the privacy of a famous client. I don't want to make a

JEANA E MANN

scene over something trivial, so I nod and move in the direction of his hand.

He escorts me to the end of the corridor but doesn't follow me further. A glance over my shoulder shows him standing in the center of the hall, arms crossed over his chest. I feel his gaze burn into my back until I reach the next junction. This time when I glance at him, he's gone. I reverse directions, head down, determined to find Nicky, and run into the hard, muscular chest of a man who smells like expensive cologne. His broad shoulders block my path. Through the holes of our masks, our gazes collide. The muscles between my legs clench at the glimpse of blue-green irises and the whiskey-over-gravel sound of his haughty, British voice.

2

HENRY

*a*fter the show in the dungeon room ends, I wander around the building, scanning the guests for long legs and silky auburn hair. I don't know why. It's not like I have the freedom to date anyone who isn't a member of royal society. Even if I had the opportunity, my appointment calendar is packed from dawn to dusk with palace duties. Free time is dedicated to the gym, an occasional charity gala, and precious sleep. Sex is a scheduled activity with a regular who has been vetted, tested for STDs, and silenced by an NDA. A relationship is dead last on my list of priorities.

"Martini, sir? Champagne? Or can I get you something from the bar?" A waiter pauses at my side, his face hidden behind the white full-face mask required for staff, similar to the kind worn by serial killers in horror movies. It lends an eerie component to the lavish fantasy.

"No, thank you." I brush past him to enter the nearest dark corridor. LED lights along the floor illuminate my path.

I bounce from one decadent sexcapade to the next. Two-way mirrors shimmer from transparent to reflective, giving the occupants privacy or inviting voyeurs to watch. The mirror across from me reveals a 1950s kitchen, a naughty house-wife, and the mailman who's about to fuck her on the linoleum. Members cluster around, anxious for the show to begin.

It's time for my meeting. I skip the exhibition and head for the reception area. As I round a corner, some woman slams into my chest, almost toppling both of us to the floor. On instinct, my fingers curl around her biceps. She places her hands on my pecs and gasps.

"Pardon me, madam. Are you okay? Did I hurt you?" My breath catches at her upturned oval face, high cheekbones, and slender nose. Behind her sequined mask, blue eyes sparkle. A ridiculous flutter dances in my gut. It's her. Nicky's redhead.

"I'm so sorry. I wasn't paying attention." She wobbles on her tall heels, still clutching my lapels. Electricity pulses through her palms and the layers of fabric between her skin and mine. A woman's touch hasn't affected me like this since prep school. Which is ridiculous. I take pride in my lack of emotions where sex is concerned.

"No worries." Let her go, Henry. With great effort, I release my hold. Her hands stay on my body for a fraction of a second too long.

"Yes. Well…" With a blush, she drops her hands to her sides. My gaze locks onto her face as she bites the fullness of her lower lip. A sweep of pink lipstick covers a mouth perfect for kisses. Except I don't do kisses. Not for her. Not for any woman. Kisses imply feelings, a luxury stolen from me by my royal birth. Even if I could kiss her, I wouldn't. Her kisses belong to Nicky. My hatred for him raises from a simmer to slow boil. Once again, he's stolen something from

me. In college, he took my fiancée. Tonight, he's stolen m
opportunity to acquire a beautiful woman.

"I'm afraid I've lost my way. Could you point me toward
reception?" I'm not lost, but I'm desperate to hear her voice
once more. I peel my gaze from her mouth. The thought of
her swollen pink lips wrapped around my dick rockets to the
top of my filthy fantasies. A step backward puts space
between us. Standing too near her stirs my blood and my
cock—a dangerous combination. The monster between my
legs is a greedy bastard. He doesn't care about Nicky or business. He just wants to get off. As much as I want to toy with
her, I can't. She's not the purpose of my visit. My meeting
with Roman requires all my attention. The future of
Androvia depends on it.

"To be honest, I'm completely turned around." Her voice
is low and smooth and made for naughty whispers in the
dark. My resolution to keep my dick in my pants waivers.
What I wouldn't give to dig my hand into that thick tangle
of hair and fuck that mouth. My erection throbs in
agreement.

"We can find the way together." I adjust the cuffs of my
tuxedo. Lord have mercy, what is she wearing? Some kind of
slinky, silky gown clings to her breasts like a second skin,
rising and falling with each breath, outlining the tight points
of her nipples. The cornflower hue contrasts with the dark
reddish-brown of her hair. Long slits on the sides reveal legs
I'd like to have wrapped around my waist. She's stunning.
Vibrant.

"I think it's this way." She points toward the next junction,
unaware of the war raging inside me. That's when her gaze
flits to the scene in the adjacent playroom. Two women in
rubber catsuits spank a man wearing nothing but a dog
collar and a smile. "Oh, my. Goodness. Um—" Her voice
fades. An adorable blush races up the graceful column of her

neck. It's an odd reaction from someone chained to a stone wall less than an hour ago.

"That's not something you see every day, is it?" My fingers clench. I'd love to wrap them around her milky throat while I fucked her from behind. To see the flush of sex spread over her alabaster breasts when she came. A laugh, something rare for me, bubbles in my chest. "They seem to be enjoying themselves."

"I don't want to watch it, but I can't look away." We stand shoulder-to-shoulder in front of the window. She cocks her head sideways to get a better perspective. "I wonder how they get into those rubber suits?"

"Lube," I reply. "Lots of it."

"Really?" She moves away from the playroom. I fall into step beside her, drawing in her scent—something sweet and floral with a hint of citrus. Her smile hits me like an unexpected punch to the gut. Mischief radiates from corner to corner. "Do you wear rubber often, sir?"

Sir? My heart skips a beat at the submissive address. Without knowing it, she's triggered my barely contained need for dominance. Beads of perspiration gather on my forehead. I clear my throat, ignoring the desire to adjust my thickening cock. "Never. But I've been in the company of those who enjoy it." A wisp of hair flutters across her cheek, begging me to brush it away. I clasp my hands behind my back.

"Is that a thing where you're from? I thought the British were stodgy and conservative."

"I'm not British."

"Oh? I'm sorry. It's just—" She's still smiling. It brightens the shadowy recesses of the corridor. Very few people smile in my world. "Your accent reminds me of Oxfordshire."

"I attended boarding school near there. Are you familiar with the area?"

"I have family in England." At the next junction, her footsteps stall. "I think we want to go left here."

It's the wrong direction, but I'm not going to tell her. The longer we're together, the more I can learn about her. I'm curious to know what she sees in Nicky, how he found her, if she enjoys power play as much as I do. "Is this your first time here?" Our shoulders brush. The accidental contact sends goosebumps racing up my arm. Does she feel it? The sexual attraction? Maybe it's wishful thinking on my part, projecting my desire on her. After all, she had another man—my sworn enemy—inside her less than an hour ago. I should mind, but I don't. In my situation, an experienced woman saves time—something I don't have a lot of these days.

"Yes." She rubs her bicep, where my sleeve grazed her bare skin.

"I— Do you— That is, are you—" My tongue trips over itself. I've never had trouble making conversation with a woman before, yet one touch from this girl has me in a tizzy. Pull yourself together, man. I swallow and try again. "Will I see you here in the future?"

"I don't know. Maybe. I'm not a member, just a guest for the evening." She quickens her pace, seeming intent to leave my company as soon as possible. I can't let that happen. Not until I know who she is. In the back of my mind, I calculate the odds of seducing this woman. Fucking her would serve two purposes—quench the ache in my balls and satisfy my vendetta against Nick the Dick.

"How else will I get to know you? Unless..." It's a bold suggestion, but I can't let her get away without knowing more. "Unless you tell me your name?"

"Breaching the NDA here is a serious offense."

"I don't play by anyone's rules but my own."

Although the hall is empty, she glances from side to side, like she's afraid someone might hear us. Her voice lowers to a whisper. "I don't know if it's true or not, but I've heard that people disappear when they talk about this place to non-members."

"Roman Menshikov and Nicky Tarnovsky don't frighten me." I dip down, placing my lips next to her ear, enjoying the clean scent of her shampoo. "I'm great at keeping secrets. In fact, if you slip your phone number into my pocket, I can keep that a secret too."

"You know I can't." The slightest of smiles twitch her lips. She likes me. I can see it in the way her body gravitates toward mine. My skin heats in anticipation. I want her in my bed, but there's so much more behind the attraction.

"But you want to." A thrill rushes through me. Victory hovers on the horizon. My mind races with plans. I need to call my personal assistant, Shasta, and have her make the necessary arrangements to add this lovely ginger girl to my roster of playmates.

"I'm not the kind of girl to ditch her date for a stranger." The rejection doesn't faze my ego. "Or have you forgotten?"

Ah, yes. The wanker. Apparently, she has no idea that I saw them in the dungeon together. I shove my hands into my pockets, wondering if I should tell her or not. After a quick internal debate, I decide to stay mum. Knowledge is power, two things I crave like an addict. "And he left you alone? Here? If you were mine, I wouldn't let you out of my sight."

"I don't need protection. I'm perfectly capable on my own." The sincerity in her voice rattles my first impressions. She seems like a genuinely lovely person, not one of Nicky's typical party girls. I don't usually go for sweet. This abrupt change in taste baffles me. What is it about her that heats my blood?

We navigate through a small crowd while I formulate a response. I can't resist touching the small of her back, guiding her through the people. Desire surges through me, the irresistible need to dominate and control the rest of her body. "And do you trust him? Your date?"

"I want to." Her answer holds a thousand clues to their relationship. Deep down, she questions Nicky's loyalty, as she should. She peers up at me. The dimple in her chin, the mole on her cheek, they sing a siren's song, luring me in, seducing me.

"But you don't?"

"Trust doesn't come easily for me." A thousand sad stories lurk behind her soft words. I want to wring the neck of every man who hurt her. She bites her lower lip. We stare at each other for a moment. Her glance drops to the floor. "And he has a reputation."

"Then you aren't serious? Please say no." In business, the best approach is often the most direct.

When she laughs, her head tips back to reveal the slender column of her throat. The delightful sound rings in my ears. "Not yet, but I'm optimistic." My hopes climb. Maybe I have a chance at stealing her for my own. The way she tucks her hair behind her ear draws my attention to her hand. Her fingers are delicate, graceful, tipped with clear nail polish, minus jewelry.

"I hope he deserves you." We start walking again. "Can I give you some advice?" I shine my best golden-boy smile. She nods. "Go with your gut instinct. It's usually right. Take me, for instance. I can tell if a person is trustworthy within five minutes of meeting them."

"Oh, really?" The bright, sunny smile returns to her face. I stare a few seconds too long, committing it to memory. "And what does your gut say about me? Am I trustworthy?"

"Are you sure you want to know?" A reluctant bob of her head persuades me to continue. "All right then." I sweep a lingering glance over the flesh revealed by the plunging neckline of her gown, the narrow nip of her waist, her flat stomach, and the slit up to her thigh. "I think you're dangerous."

"What? Not me." She bats her sooty eyelashes, pressing a hand to her heart in a comical yet seductive impression of a southern belle. "Surely, you're mistaken, sir."

"I would trust you with my car keys but never my heart." Her mouth drops open to speak. I lift a hand to silence her. "That's not an insult. It's a compliment. I'm just saying I have a feeling you could get under a man's skin and stay there."

"Am I getting under yours?" The mischief returns to her grin. She cocks a slender eyebrow, daring me to answer. My heart skips a beat.

"Are you flirting with me, angel?" I block her path through the next doorway with my shoulders. It's a subtle form of domination, one I can't help. The longer I'm around her, the more I want to back her up against the wall, pin her arms over her head, and make her beg me to fuck her.

"Of course not." Dimples deepen alongside her lips. "And I'm not an angel. Not even close."

"You wouldn't lie to me, would you?"

"Never."

Our gazes catch for a handful of seconds. I blow out a heavy breath, aware of my cock straining against my trousers, tempted to find the nearest restroom and jack off to relieve the throbbing pressure. If I were a cautious man, I'd walk away. Lucky for her, I've never been able to ignore a challenge. Her denial makes me want her even more. "I understand why you won't give me your number, but can I give you mine? In case you decide to dump your boyfriend?" As a royal, this violates every rule of protocol, but for her, I'm willing to make an exception.

3

EVERLY

The enigmatic gentleman withdraws an ink pen from the inside pocket of his tuxedo and writes his phone number on my palm in neat, square numbers. His fingers are warm and commanding and linger on my skin before pulling away. I can't help imagining how his touch would feel on my breasts.

"Did you like it?" He nods toward the red marks left on my wrists by the shackles. A touch of gravel roughens the haughtiness of his accent. It's the kind of voice that could charm the panties off a woman—this woman. At a different time, under different circumstances, I could fall head over heels for this guy.

"It was unique. In a good way, I guess." I shift my stance and fight the urge to hide my hands behind my back. The sensation of helplessness, the weight of the restraints, and the chill of steel against my skin awakened something dark inside my soul. Rourke, my best friend, says I need to push my boundaries more often. I stifle a giggle. I don't think she meant this. Or maybe she did. After all, her husband created this club.

"Restraints can be liberating when used properly." He brushes a thumb over the underside of my wrist; reverent and gentle. Goosebumps ripple up my forearm.

"Liberating? Isn't that defeating the purpose?"

"Not at all." His touch eases from my skin. "If you don't feel empowered by the exchange, your partner isn't doing it right."

Fantasies of being tied up and ravished by this man clutter my thoughts. The moisture evaporates from my mouth. Although my experience with Nicky was novel, it left me unsated. Like one bite of a decadent dessert leaves me hungering for more. Before I can give voice to my feelings, a group filters into the hall with us. It's just as well. I don't need to confide my sexual dissatisfaction to a complete stranger. To give the newcomers room, I step to the side. One of the passing men bumps my shoulder. The accidental contact pushes me into the stranger. My palms splay on his chest for a second time.

"Careful." Tanned skin contrasts with the starched front of his white silk shirt. My gaze continues to his neat goatee and square jaw. He's hot, in a James Bond meets David Beckham kind of way. Heaven knows I've always been a sucker for a blond.

"I'm so sorry. Again..." My voice trails off. I drop my hands to my sides, curling my fingers into fists against the lingering heat of his body. Is it normal for a man to be that warm? I bite my lower lip, choking back the urge to babble excuses for touching him twice.

"The pleasure is all mine." The way his voice draws out the final word, like he's thinking naughty things, stirs butterflies in my stomach. From behind the mask, his gaze makes a slow perusal of my body. Heat climbs up my neck and settles in my face. "I'm happy to be of service."

Although I'm wearing a floor-length gown, I feel naked. My nipples poke through the clingy silk of the dress. Thank goodness I have the mask to protect my identity. I lift a hand to touch the ribbon holding it in place; his intense stare seems to burn through it.

"I really should find my date." With every passing second, my heart rate escalates. What is it about this man that puts me on edge? What if he knows me? Or even worse—my father? My palms begin to sweat. Coming here was such a bad idea. If someone recognizes me, the damage to the McElroy name would be irreparable. Then again, most of the people here are famous. A breach of confidentiality would be damaging for everyone.

"His loss is my gain, it seems." The stranger paces at my side. We make small talk as we wander through the labyrinth of hallways. He pauses to open a door for me. I pass by, ignoring the flip of my stomach at the nearness of his body to mine, because I'm here with Nicky. Nicky, who sprinted out of the dungeon after sex tonight like his tail was on fire. Nicky, who never answers my calls or texts. Nicky, who's coming out of a playroom with another woman, tie askew, shirt untucked, hair ruffled, looking guilty as sin.

HENRY

"Ah, there you are." Nicky exits the playroom, twitches the knot of his tie, and extends his hands toward my companion. The years haven't changed him. Same cover model features. Same athletic build. Same dickish expression. A young woman slides out the door behind him, tugging down her skirt, hustling out of sight. Same cheating bastard. My heart breaks for the beauty at my side.

The smile drops from her face. "I've been waiting for you to come back for, like, forty-five minutes." Uncertainty in her voice stirs my compassion. Her boyfriend likes to play games, to find a person's most significant weakness then use it against them. No one knows that better than me.

"I told you to meet me in reception." Even though Nicky's an American citizen, a hint of Russian accents his speech, a remnant of his teen years in Prague. His gaze flits from her to me. An arrogant smirk curls one side of his mouth as he recognizes me. He drops a hand to cup her ass, a blatant gesture meant to show his claim on her. I bite the inside of my cheek, fighting the urge to punch him in the nose.

"No. You said to wait." Her brow furrows. "I'm sure of it."

I jump into the discussion. Despite his hand on her ass. Despite the fact that he was inside her less than an hour ago. Despite the voice in my head warning me not to get involved. "It's my fault. I was lost. She helped me find the way." I keep my gaze leveled on Nicky. He knows it's me behind the mask. In the back of my head, I scroll through all the numerous ways to punish him for hurting this woman, for ruining my engagement to Kitty, destroying our friendship, humiliating me. My list of grievances is a mile long. Now, however, isn't the time to let emotions rule my actions. Revenge requires thoughtful planning and cool diligence, skills imparted on me since birth. "She's been excellent company."

"Has she?" Nicky's jaw tightens.

"Absolutely." I should feel guilty, but I don't. Fuck him. He doesn't deserve a beauty like her.

"That's because she's an amazing woman." At least he recognizes her worth. He bends to place a kiss on her temple, drawing her tighter into his side. His words are directed to her, but his gaze remains locked with mine. "Please forgive me. What about you, darling? Where have you been? It doesn't take forty-five minutes to find me."

"I came straight here, even though Achilles sent me in the wrong direction. I think he was trying to distract me from finding you." The flush of anger brightens her cheeks. She squirms out of his grasp. "Who was that girl?"

From the glare on Nicky's face and the furrow of the redhead's brow, an argument is about to erupt. My respect for her climbs a notch. At least she calls him out on his bad behavior. I try to hold back my grin of satisfaction at the signs of unrest in their relationship. Rousting Nicky from her life might be easier than anticipated. Not too easy, I hope. He needs to suffer.

A panel in the wall slides open, revealing a secret corridor. A club employee steps into the hall and gestures for me to follow him. "Pardon me, sir. The Grand Master is ready to see you. Both of you." He nods toward Nicky.

"We'll discuss this later, darling." Nicky nudges his date toward the exit. "I'll get a car for you."

Her eyebrows lower until they reach the edge of her mask. "Don't bother." The wavy ends of her hair bounce as she tries to go around him. How is it possible for her to be lovelier in anger than during sex? The combination of the two would be the culmination of all my darkest fantasies. Her wrath orchestrated by my whim. Fire eddies in my veins at the thought.

"No need. I have a car waiting." Seizing the opportunity to make Nicky look bad, I step between them. "My driver can take you anywhere you need to go."

4

EVERLY

*T*he stranger is clean, crisp and provocative, from the top of his spiky blond hair to the tips of his glossy black shoes. Behind the mask, his eyes glitter, taunting and tempting me. I want to rip off the strip of leather to see the unobstructed perfection of his face. He watches in silence as I struggle with the war between my head and heart.

"I'll walk you outside." Nicky herds me away from the stranger.

"Not until you tell me the truth." I plant my feet. My heart wants to believe the best of him, but his track record suggests otherwise. As the stranger noted earlier, I need to follow my gut instincts, and my gut suspects the worst.

Nicky grips my elbow, steering me toward the exit, but I can't leave. Not until I have answers. "Don't make a scene. People are staring." He deflects the blame to me, something my ex-husband used to do when he had been caught in the wrong.

"I don't care." No one is staring but the golden mystery man. His quiet gaze is more unnerving than Nicky's philandering. I smooth my hair away from my face, trying to remain calm. My temper, however, has always been a challenge to control. "Let them look."

"Not now." The harshness in Nicky's voice causes me to flinch. "I can't talk to you when you're like this."

"You're mad? At me?" My skin heats as Nicky's gray eyes bounce from me to the stranger and back again. Incredulity bubbles in my chest. "I haven't done anything wrong."

"I didn't say you had." His tone is bored, almost cruel.

"You're acting like an ass."

"That's because I *am* an ass, darling."

"I'm not your darling." An hour ago, my feelings for Nicky bordered on adoration, but now that the glow of sex has faded, in the face of his unfaithfulness, I know better. I know better, but I need to hear him admit his infidelity. He pauses to examine his reflection in the glass of the framed print next to the door. My temperature climbs, along with the volume of my voice. "Don't patronize me."

"Calm down, sweets." He stares at me like I'm out of my mind. In truth, I feel crazy. Crazy for putting up with his bullshit.

"You have her lipstick on your mouth." He drags a thumb over his lips to remove the evidence of kisses from another woman. I storm past him, throw open the exit door. It clangs against the wall and bounces back, almost hitting me in the nose. The whole time, the stranger's stare bores into me. He follows us outside, moving to speak with his driver while I glare at my date.

"Hey, hey." In the damp alley, Nicky grabs my biceps, the same way the stranger had done to keep us from crashing into each other. I have a quick, inappropriate memory of how hard and warm the stranger is. His touch had been comforting, reassuring, while Nicky's grasp fuels my temper.

"Let go." I yank my arms free of his hold.

His hands fall to his sides. The tone of his voice softens. "I don't want to fight with you." With a gentle touch, he smooths my hair over my shoulder. "You have nothing to worry about. If anyone should be upset, it's me. That man—" His chin jerks in the direction of the stranger. "He's morally bankrupt." His fingers glide along my back. Sweet, charming Nicky returns. Only this time, I see through his pretty words.

"Don't." I exhale, eager for privacy in the interior of the Maybach. No man is worth this kind of trouble.

"I'm not. I'm just saying that you should stay away from him. We have a history. I don't like to talk about it, but he fucked me over once." He pulls me back into his embrace, placing his lips next to my ear. "You know I'm falling for you, right? I could be in love with you so easily."

More than anything, I want to believe a man can love me, that I have value to someone. My ex-husband betrayed me in the worst way and chose his mistress over our marriage. I can't go through that again. Nicky wraps an arm around my waist. I lean into his chest. He kisses me, flicking his tongue between my lips. I close my eyes, thinking of the stranger, wondering how he tastes. Like mint? Or with a hint of scotch?

When I open my eyes, he's staring at us from the opened door of his limousine. Butterflies twitter in my stomach. For the stranger. Not for Nicky. How is that possible? How can I have feelings for Nicky one minute then feel such a strong attraction to a man I don't even know? Each passing second with Nicky reinforces the answer. I'm not ready for a relationship. Not with a man known for breaking hearts. Not with him. Maybe not with anyone.

"We're both on edge tonight." Nicky's eyes follow mine and narrow when he sees the blond staring back at me. "Go home. Get some rest. We'll talk tomorrow."

"Thank you for the lift," I smile at the stranger, ignoring Nicky, and slide into the cool interior of the car.

"It's my pleasure." The man nudges Nicky aside then bends down like he's going to kiss me. He's close enough to smell the clean scent of his shampoo. My heart races around my chest, pinging off my ribs. He flicks the hem of my dress inside the Maybach. "Give your address to the driver." He straightens and shuts the door, enveloping me in a cloud of quiet luxury.

"Where to, madam?" The masked driver addresses my reflection in his rearview mirror.

"Wait." I shift to the edge of the soft leather seat. "How do I know you won't tell anyone where I live?"

"My employer would never allow such a breach of confidentiality," the driver says, his gaze averted from my masked face.

"Can you tell me his name?"

"No, madam. Confidentiality works both ways." The defiant set of his jaw reflects back at me through the rearview mirror.

"I see." I glance down at the phone number on my hand. The ink is smudged and unreadable. It's probably just as well. The thought of my comfortable bed inside the refuge of my apartment overrides the need for more questions. I rattle off my address and settle into the supple butterscotch seat.

Outside the car, the broad shoulders of the golden stranger disappear into the building. Even from a distance, his posture is regal, almost arrogant. Who is he? Why can't I stop thinking about him? I shake my head and exhale a long breath. Obviously, this thing with Nicky isn't going to work out. Our relationship is doomed, but I can't seem to let him go. If I do, I'll have to admit that I picked the wrong man. Again.

5

HENRY

"$\mathcal{W}$elcome back, Your Royal Highness." Inside his office, Roman Menshikov, Grand Master of the Devil's Playground franchise and the exiled prince of Kitzeh, greets me. His handshake is firm, the kind of grip that instills fear in lesser men. A custom tuxedo and unshaven jaw give him the perfect mix of uncivilized yet polished, symbolic of a powerful billionaire who doesn't give a fuck what anyone thinks of him. The black mask covering his eyes adds to his sinister air.

Nick hovers at his elbow. "We got off to a rocky start this evening, Henry. Let's start over." He extends his hand. I avoid it. Tosser. I don't care if he's Roman's younger brother and business partner. He can suck my dick. After a beat, he flexes his fingers and drops his fist to his side.

"Thank you for having me, Roman." I try to shift into business mode, but my thoughts remain with Nick's gorgeous redhead. She was so beautiful in her clingy silk dress and sky-high heels as she tried to hide her hurt over his behavior. I glance around the paneled office the two men share, taking in the security camera on the ceiling, the matching desks, and the priceless modern art on the walls. "Are we allowed to remove our masks in here?"

"Yes. Absolutely. Make yourself comfortable. Would you like something to drink?" In one smooth motion, Roman tugs the mask from his head and tucks it into the breast pocket of his tuxedo jacket, silk strings dangling.

I breathe a sigh of relief and follow suit. "Not right now. Thanks."

Roman takes a seat behind the desk, leans back in his chair, and steeples his fingers in front of him. "Tell me. What do you think about our club? We'd love to have you as a permanent member."

"It's intriguing, but not for me. I have more—specific—tastes." Call it whatever you want—a side effect of my damaged childhood, lingering hatred for my overbearing mother, or just a general need to dominate—but the thought of a beautiful girl on her knees begging me to fuck her is enough to make my cock jerk to attention. And I'd prefer to do it without an audience.

"Still fond of whips and handcuffs?" Nick asks, lifting an eyebrow.

"Any fool can chain a woman to a wall," I reply quietly. "What I do requires skill." How do I explain the delicate process of stripping away a woman's will and bending it to my own? A shallow man like Nicky could never understand the amount of time, consideration, and proficiency required.

Nick opens his mouth to reply, but a scathing look from Roman causes him to bite his tongue. It seems his lips are still firmly attached to his big brother's ass. Roman taps a fingernail on the surface of his desk, assessing the tension between his sibling and me. "What have you done, Nicky?"

"What makes you think I've done anything?" His eyebrows shoot up, feigning shock.

"Because I know you." The muscles in Roman's jaw tighten. "If my brother has done anything to offend you, Prince Henrich, I apologize."

He doesn't know. No one does. As far as the world is concerned, my engagement to Lady Catherine Clayton ended by mutual agreement, not because I found my best mate between her legs. I might be arrogant and opportunistic, but I've always been a gentleman. And a gentleman doesn't ruin the reputation of a woman, no matter how unsavory or salacious the affront. Therefore, I've kept the secret, biding my time until I can repay them for their insult.

"How is Kitty Cat anyway?" Nick slouches in his chair, wearing the same goddam smirk he's had since college. "I haven't seen her in ages."

"I wouldn't know." Before I accepted Roman's invitation to the club, I knew Nicky would be a part of the meeting, and I swore to myself that I wouldn't let him get under my skin. Despite my promise, pressure builds inside my chest. It wouldn't take much for me to launch across the room and strangle him with his stupid lavender tie. "We aren't exactly close these days."

"What a shame. I thought for sure you'd patch things up and marry her anyway." Delight dances in his eyes. The years might have passed, but he's still the same bloke who burst into my dorm on the first day of university with a bottle of scotch in one hand, a box of Cuban cigars in the other, and the panties of the dean's wife stuffed into his trouser pocket. "You have to be married to claim the throne, right? Kitty was really looking forward to becoming your queen."

"Thankfully, my father is in good health." And living life to the fullest with his mistress. I have plenty of years to find the right woman.

"Nick, zip it, or you can leave." Steel edges the words of Roman's warning. Nicky sighs and rolls his eyes. I stifle a chuckle. His big brother has him on a very tight leash. Good for him. Roman clears his throat, tilting his chair until the back hits the wall. "I'm sorry to rush, Henry, but it's been one hell of an evening, and I have someone special waiting for me. Can we get down to business?"

"Please." My need to punish his younger brother will have to wait. Besides, it seems Roman is doing a great job of making his life uncomfortable.

"After our discussion last night, I've been looking into your problem, and I think I have an answer." We've been meeting in secret for the past month, brainstorming options to liberate our countries from unfortunate circumstances.

"I'm all ears." I try to remain calm. For the past several years, my father has reigned terror down on Androvia from his throne. He's ignored the steady flow of heroin through our country and rebel uprisings to line his pockets, oblivious to the misery of his subjects. Once I wear the crown, this shit is going to stop, and Roman is my ticket to success. Although my reign won't arrive for at least another decade, I've been insinuating myself into royal politics, so I'll be ready.

"Don McElroy is your problem."

I shove back in my chair, too stunned to speak. Don McElroy is a war hero, two-term Vice President of the United States, celebrated humanitarian, and recipient of the Congressional Medal of Honor. "Are you sure?" I ask once my voice returns.

"My sources are reliable," Roman replies. "He's facilitating the movement of drugs—and God knows what else—through your country into mine, and into the hands of eager

European clients. From what I've learned, your father has chosen to turn a blind eye to this travesty as long as he gets a cut of the action."

Anger swells inside me until my skin feels like it's going to burst. "They've got to be stopped." Memories of war-torn villages, drug-addicted citizens, and opulent palace parties turn my stomach. As long as my parents can dine on caviar and lobster every evening, they don't give two shits about the people on the streets. "I'll do anything necessary."

"I'm working on it from the inside." Nicky jumps back into the conversation, acting like we haven't been at odds since he broke up my engagement. Fucker. "I hope to have details soon."

"I'll do everything in my power to help you. Nicky has infiltrated McElroy's camp, and he's making good progress. McElroy is nervous. He's putting pressure on me to ship weapons to his guerillas on your border." Roman raises a hand in the air. "Don't worry. I've refused." He rests his elbows on the desk and leans forward. "All I need is your word of honor. Persuade your father to sign an alliance with Kitzeh and put a stop to this madness."

"Done." One small country is subject to the whims of invaders and opportunists. Two small countries conjoined have twice the protection, twice the military presence, twice the power. "Excuse me for stating the obvious, but your family was ousted from Kitzeh a few decades ago." The rebel invasion had slaughtered the king and queen, leaving the infant Prince Roman to be raised in secrecy. "How can you guarantee Kitzeh's compliance?"

"Leave the details to me. Just know that I have troops in place, as we speak, waiting for the go-ahead. In a few days, they're going to storm the capital and take back what's mine. The real question is whether or not you can divert your father's attention long enough for us to make this move?"

"Absolutely." I listen to Roman's plan. King Gustav has been too busy cavorting on the royal yacht in Santorini to dwell on boring matters of state. His distraction presents a window of opportunity. Roman's armies will close up Kitzeh's borders, running the traffickers into a dead end. They'll have no choice but to circumvent Androvia's steep border mountains and flowing rivers, ridding my precious homeland of its menace.

"In the meantime, I need you to sit tight, Your Highness. And watch your back." Roman stands. "There are rumors that the Androvian throne is in jeopardy. If McElroy is indeed at the head of this scourge, he won't hesitate to eliminate anyone who stands between him and victory. Your problems run much deeper than you think." With a sharp tug, he adjusts the cuffs of his shirt beneath his tuxedo jacket. Brilliant diamond cufflinks wink in the light. "It's important for you to keep our affiliation quiet until we get him under control."

"Agreed." Few men have my admiration, but this guy is in a class by himself. No one messes with Roman Menshikov. My success is guaranteed with him as a partner. "Androvia will help in any way we can."

"Excellent. I have a feeling we're going to make history together." Roman's gaze bores into me. "I hope you're ready for the ride."

"I'm looking forward to it," I reply.

We walk toward the door. Roman withdraws his mask from his pocket and slips it into place, nodding for me to do the same. He hesitates with a hand on the door handle. "Before we go, I wonder if I might ask you a favor?"

"Anything."

"A young woman died under suspicious circumstances last night—Lavender Cunningham. She was an event planner for my company. Perhaps you've heard of her?"

I shake my head, wondering what this has to do with me. "Her name sounds familiar. I wasn't aware of her passing. My condolences."

"Thank you, Your Highness." The shrug of his shoulders reveals little emotion. "The police are interested in my whereabouts at the time of her death. As you know, I was with you last night, discussing strategies. I can't give the investigators an alibi without revealing our relationship, and I don't want to drag you into this shitstorm." We don our masks, preparing to re-enter the decadent playground. He opens the door and gestures for me to step out of the office. "If our names are linked, the entire plan, as well as our lives, will be in jeopardy. McElroy isn't known for being sympathetic to his adversaries."

"Agreed." The repercussions would be catastrophic. "But if you need me to vouch for you, I will."

He lifts a hand into the air, palm facing forward. "I'll deal with it. I just want you to be aware in case they come to you. For the time being, I think it's best for both of us to remain silent."

"Your consideration is appreciated. I'll take precautions. If the situation changes, let me know. I'll do whatever I can for you." While we walk, I text Shasta, asking her to erase all traces of Roman's name from my appointment calendar and schedules. She answers right away, even though it's past midnight, leading me to wonder if my personal assistant ever sleeps.

"Let's hope it doesn't come to that."

Now that Roman is indebted to me, I'm emboldened to ask for a favor. "Before I go, I was wondering about the woman you were with tonight, Nikolay."

Nicky's gray eyes narrow. "What about her?"

"I want her." Circumspection has never been one of my traits. In my experience, few people have the balls to deny the request of a prince. "And I'm going to take her from you."

"Why? So you can turn her into one of your zombie lovers? I don't think so." Nick lifts his chin. The playfulness leaves his gaze. His refusal heightens my curiosity about the leggy beauty. "She only came here tonight because of my considerable persuasive skills, not because she's submissive."

"Maybe. Or we could consider it repayment for the woman you stole from me." I match his gaze in intensity.

"That's not possible." Roman shakes his dark head and steps between us. "I'm sorry, but we don't reveal identities. Not even for you. And this woman isn't the type to be owned." His relaxed demeanor doesn't fool me. Beneath the sharp lines of his black tuxedo, he's coiled for action, like a cobra about to strike. We resume our walk, shoulder-to-shoulder in the wide corridor. Nikolay trails behind us. Knowing he's back there makes the hairs stand on the nape of my neck. The last time I turned my back on him, he betrayed me. A mistake I'll never make again. "If you're interested in an anonymous companion for your next visit, one of my matchmakers would be happy to match your profile to one of our members."

"I appreciate the offer, but I can find my own dates," I reply, unable to hide a hint of arrogance. My royal title acts as human catnip for the ladies. "I'm interested in only her."

"Giving out names—even one—undermines the integrity of this club." Nick's steps ahead to open the next door. The angry clench of his jaw fuels my intrigue. In my experience, he was never proprietary over any woman. What keeps him interested in the redhead other than her undeniable beauty and winning personality? "Violation of the NDA has serious consequences. Even for us."

"Of course. I understand." I nod, far from satisfied with

his answer. Defeat has never been an option for me. "She should be easy enough to track down."

"It would be in everyone's best interest if you walk away from her." Roman's icy tone cements my resolve. The smile falls from Nicky's lips. He doesn't want me to know this woman, making her all the more desirable. I'm going to find her and take her, and I hope he hates me for it.

6

EVERLY

a month passes, and my anger at Nicky fades. He continues to call, and I continue to answer. I have a handful of events scheduled in the upcoming weeks—events Nicky promised to attend as my escort. Charitable donations at my family fundraisers climb twenty percent when he's present. He might be a dick, but he knows how to pry money out of a rich person's wallet better than anyone I've ever met. I need to suck it up. After all, he's handsome, amusing, and well-connected. I resolve to stick with him a little longer. Just until my string of charity events finish. Then, we can go our separate directions.

Sometimes I catch him gazing into the distance, brows furrowed, like he's thinking of someone else. Those looks are enough to remind me this isn't real. We're fucking each other to pass the time until the right person comes along. So, I turn a blind eye to the way he hides his phone screen, leaves the room to take late-night calls, and disappears for days at a time.

Tonight is the evening of the Medallion-Hearst Charity Auction. The wealthiest people in New York are here, wallets in hand, eager to pay big dollars for the rescue of human trafficking victims. It's a topic dear to my heart. One I've devoted my life to. And I depend on Nicky to work his magic on the wealthiest of them.

I survey The Plaza Hotel ballroom with a critical eye, taking in the white linens, towering floral centerpieces, and auction items on display. Laughter floats above the music. Everyone seems to be having a great time. As I scan the space, a tall man with spiky blond hair catches my eye. Heat races up my neck. Is it him? The guy from the Devil's Playground? My heart pounds. I place a hand on the wall for support.

"Sorry I'm late, darling. I can only stay a minute." Nicky's empty smile interrupts my line of sight. "A business emergency. You understand."

"Sure." The light from the crystal chandeliers bounces off his platinum cufflinks. I'm too distracted by the blond man to express any disappointment. I strain to catch a glimpse of him over Nicky's shoulder. "Is everything okay?"

"It will be." A whiff of his cologne teases my nose as he bends down to plant a kiss on my cheek. He straightens, his gaze sweeping across the ballroom. "You've done an excellent job. You should be very proud."

"Thank you." The sincerity in his compliment brings a second rush of heat into my face. I'm being paranoid. Maybe the coolness in his eyes is due to stress over his work conflict. Although I've never seen Nicky stressed since Rourke introduced us. I want to ask, but I'm afraid of the answer, so I change the subject. "Is that the blond man from the Devil's Playground?"

"Where?" Nicky's head snaps up.

"Over there. Black tuxedo, black shirt, black tie. With a brunette in a green dress."

The lines across his forehead deepen in a brief scowl. "If it's him, I couldn't tell you without violating the club NDA. Why? Is he bothering you? I told you to stay away from him."

"Never mind. It's probably just someone who looks like him." He's right. I don't need more distractions in my life. Instead, I focus on the perfection of the venue, the strains of classical music from the string quartet, and the laughter of the guests. Manhattan's most elegant have turned out in record numbers to support the McElroy Foundation. When I look back to Nicky, my father is in his place and the Russian is gone.

"Did I just see Nicky leave? I was hoping to speak with him." As always, my father's voice booms with quiet authority.

"He had a business emergency." I follow the statement with a pleasant smile to prevent more questions and to mask the twist of rejection in my gut. Nicky didn't even say good-bye. Deep down, I know there's more behind his departure than business. I don't know why I feel so sad about it. He's not my soulmate. I don't even like him.

Father inclines his head toward the blond man. "Is that Prince Heinrich of Androvia?"

"I don't know." I've heard the name before. His reputation as a shrewd businessman is overshadowed by the intrigue of his royal title. Admirers cluster around him, eager for the attention of a future king. My heart skips a beat at the sight of his regal profile—a straight nose, strong chin and forehead, a jaw carved from granite. He *could* be the golden stranger. I bite my lower lip and pray it's not him. "We've never met."

"Yes. I'm sure it's him." The ice clinks against the sides of his glass as he prepares for another sip. "I'd like to speak to him. Come with me. I'll introduce you."

"No." My answer arrives too quickly. An encounter with someone who might be from the Devil's Playground rattles my composure. Father lifts an eyebrow. I clear my throat and try to soften the refusal. "Maybe later."

Sensing our attention, the prince turns to face us. My gaze connects with his. The bottom drops out of my stomach. For the span of a heartbeat, I can't breathe. Is it him? I try to picture his face with a mask covering his eyes. The brunette at his side places a hand on his forearm. Jealousy prickles along the back of my neck. I don't know why. I'm not interested, yet I can't stop thinking about him at night when I'm alone in bed. An incoming group of guests blocks my view. When the crowd thins, the prince and his companion are gone.

"You and your mother have done an amazing job tonight. The work you're doing here is important, honey. I'm so proud of you." Father's words draw me back to the shattered remains of my family. He knows I'm angry with him for the chaos he's caused.

"Your tie is crooked." I grab the ends of Father's bowtie and straighten them. In the past, his words of praise meant the world to me. Now the compliment rings hollow like our relationship. He smiles down at me. I concentrate on the tie. Having him here is comforting and confusing. He used to be a rock of stability in my life. The day I met his mistress changed everything.

"Thank you, dear." The warmth of his arm heats my shoulder as he gives me a hug. "I guess you're speaking to me again. Does this mean I'm forgiven?"

"Not even a little." Although my tone is flat and my expression is neutral, I'm seething inside. His adulterous affair with Lavender Carpenter was a personal attack on the stability of our family unit and a blow to my heart. "I'm not sure I'll ever be able to trust you again."

"Don't be ridiculous." Lines of good humor bracket his mouth. Most people think we look alike with our blue eyes and tall stature. Right now, he seems like a stranger. "I'm the same man I've always been."

"Not to me." Tears burn my eyes. I fight them away. "You used to be kind and compassionate and honest." Those traits got him elected to two terms in the White House. I was so proud of him. "What happened? Is it Mom? Don't you love her anymore?" The thought of my mother's potential anguish blossoms into an ache beneath my ribs. She doesn't know about the affair, and now I'm complicit in his deception. His secret keeps me awake at night, contemplating the ripple effects of his infidelity.

"You've just described every loser in the history of mankind. Those characteristics don't accomplish goals." A waiter arrives with a glass of liquor on a silver tray for him. The conversation lulls long enough for Father to place his empty glass on the tray and claim the new one. "Haven't you learned anything from me?"

Random acts of Father's kindness spin in a loop amid my childhood memories—his kisses on my scraped knees, the protective grasp of his fingers on my five-year-old hand as we crossed the street, his soothing words after a nightmare. Those are the actions of a caring human being. The recollection of his hand on Lavender Cunningham's ass taints those memories.

"Yes," I reply. "I've learned never to trust you—or any man —again."

* * *

THE NEXT MORNING, I awaken with a headache. In need of

caffeine and aspirin, I throw on a pair of yoga pants and a T-shirt and walk down the block to the coffee shop. The throbbing between my temples increases at the corner newsstand. Nicky's face splashes across the tabloids. Each photo depicts him in the arms of the same sexy Hollywood starlet. She's filming a movie in New York City and hitting the clubs at night. Their smiling faces taunt me. I shouldn't be devastated, but I am. The wound in my chest throbs. He found someone else. Someone younger. Someone prettier. Someone more famous. Someone who isn't me.

I know it's ridiculous—these feelings of hurt and rejection. We should have ended things a long time ago. It doesn't make the sting any worse. Like a fool, I hung on to him, more frightened of being alone than unhappy. The funny thing? I'm mad at myself for allowing this to happen.

The longer I think about his betrayal and the way he ghosted me last night, the angrier I become. I'm tired of men disrespecting me. My ex-husband's affair, my father's adultery, Nicky's cheating—the three deceptions blend together inside my head. I down a double shot of espresso and grab a taxi, hoping to put an end to this charade once and for all.

Nicky lives in a swanky tower of condominiums on 67th Street. The front desk clerk buzzes his apartment to announce my arrival. My palms sweat on the elevator ride to the top. I have no idea what I'm going to say when I get there. Only that I deserve better treatment, and I won't allow him to disrespect me again. By the time I reach his apartment, my temper is on the uptick. He answers the door wearing a pair of black boxer shorts and nothing else.

"This is unexpected." Instead of inviting me inside, he blocks the door, forcing me to stand in the hall. "Did we have a breakfast appointment or something?"

"No." This is such a bad idea. I'm tempted to sprint back to the elevators. Instead, I draw in a deep breath to bolster my courage. "I want you to explain this." I shove the tabloid magazine into his chest.

The paper crackles as he glances at the cover then smirks. "That's a great photo. My hair looks phenomenal. Did you see this, babe?" He hands the paper over his shoulder to the woman behind him. It's the starlet. She's wearing panties and his tuxedo shirt, the same one he had on last night. My humiliation is complete.

"Oh, nice photos," the girl says. "I love free publicity." Her enormous hazel eyes rove over my rumpled T-shirt and yoga pants. "Who's this?"

"I'm Everly McElroy. I've been sleeping with Nicky, too. Did he tell you, or is he lying to you as well?"

"Yeah, I know. I don't mind." With a sleepy smile, she wraps her fingers around his bicep and tugs him backward. "Come back to bed, baby. She can come too."

"No, thank you."

"Come on. Don't be mad." Nicky's words lack conviction.

"It didn't have to end like this. You know that, right?" I stand in front of him, feeling like my chest has been ripped open, and wait for an explanation that never arrives. After an uncomfortable beat, I shake my head. Without a backward glance, I flee to the street. A cool breeze rolls up from the road, swirling my hair into my eyes. I press a hand to my stomach, fighting a wave of frustration. My life is falling apart.

7

HENRY

*F*or the next month, my duties as a prince are demanding. After the meeting with Roman at the Devil's Playground, I jet off to London for tea with the Prince of Wales then cross the globe to preside over the opening of a new vineyard in Tuscany. Between a Boston polo match and a royal wedding in Sweden, I deliver food and supplies to Somalian refugees. Manhattan charities beg for my presence. And I manage to fit a few in. The relentless royal schedule fills my days. In the mornings, however, I wake up with an erection tenting the sheets and visions of long auburn hair wrapped around my shaft. Memories of Nicky's date continue to haunt me. Prudent judgment warns me to let his mystery girl go, but I can't. Mostly because she's unattainable. For a man who can have anything he wants, she's become the ultimate prize.

On my first morning back in Manhattan, Shasta drops an

unmarked envelope onto my hotel desk. She's been at my side for years, acting as my most trusted advisor.

"What's this?" I ask, shoving aside my laptop.

"It's the information you requested about the girl."

"Ah, yes." The girl. Long legs, perfect tits, and a smile that could light up the darkest of skies. It takes all of my self-control to hide my excitement. "You found her?"

"When have I ever failed you, Your Royal Highness?" She rolls her expressive brown eyes behind the blue plastic frames of her glasses. My life would be shambles without her calm capability and organizational skills. When I gave her the task of finding my fantasy woman, I never expected her to succeed, but I should have known better. Shasta always comes through for me.

"Never, but there's always a first time," I reply, teasing. Taking the envelope in my hands, I turn it over a few times. The cadence of my heart escalates. For all I know, this woman could be a grocery clerk, a barista, or a dog walker. The possibilities are thrilling. Not that it matters. My interest in her is purely sexual. "Have you read the contents?" I wave the envelope.

"Of course. I had to know what kind of woman requires three private detectives to find."

"And?" I lift an eyebrow.

"Now, I understand." Shasta clasps her hands in front of her, waiting for my next command. "She's quite unique."

I'm as excited as a child on Christmas Eve. Taking my time, I break the seal and fold over the flap, drawing out the pleasure of the unknown. Documents, photographs, and magazine articles flutter onto the desk. My breath catches in my throat. The mystery girl stares back at me from an eight-by-ten glossy photograph through wide blue eyes. I drink in every inch of her oval-shaped face, her slender nose, and bee-stung lips. It's her.

Everly McElroy was the stunning beauty chained to Roman Menshikov's dungeon wall. In a million years, I never would have guessed her identity. This isn't your average woman off the street. This woman has raised millions of dollars to fight sex trafficking, lobbied to change laws, and rallied to protect those less fortunate than herself. In fact, I attended one of her events last night. I dig through the photographs until I find one that catches my attention. She's riding a gray mare, her round ass encased in snug white breeches, a blue ribbon in her hand and a smile on her face. It's her smile that captivates me most: bright, sunny, and carefree.

I lean back in my chair to contemplate the implications. Not only is she the star of my wet dreams, but she's also the daughter of my adversary. The consequences of any contact between us could be catastrophic. On the other hand, she might provide valuable insight into Don McElroy's schemes. No wonder Nicky didn't want me to know her. I tap a fingernail on the desk. Complications like her provide an intriguing layer to the tedious duties of royalty.

At my elbow, Shasta waits patiently, hands clasped in front of her severe blue suit. I scribble a message on a blank piece of paper and hand it to her. "Send Ms. McElroy a dozen red roses—make that two dozen—and give her this note. Clear my schedule for tonight. I'll be going out."

EVERLY

The clock at the Devil's Playground strikes midnight. I'm grateful to say goodbye to such a disappointing day. I perch on the edge of a chaise lounge, rise to leave, and sit back down again. It's been less than twenty-four hours since Nicky humiliated me at his apartment door. Now I'm sitting at his sex club, waiting on a man who may or may not be the

Crown Prince of Androvia to ravish my body. It's too crazy to comprehend.

This afternoon, a handwritten invitation from the masked stranger arrived at my apartment along with the biggest roses I've ever seen. Throughout the day, I've changed my mind a dozen times. Who does something like this? Yesterday, I would've laughed at the suggestion, but tonight, I'm too hurt and angry at the men in my life to care. All I want to do is forget them. If screwing a stranger does the trick, I'm all for it. This is the perfect scenario. No names. No faces. Just sex.

The heels of my shoes echo on the marble floor as I pace from one side to the other, a glass of chardonnay in hand. This special playroom is dubbed the Sultan's Lair and mimics the boudoir of a sheik. Sheer scarves cascade from the ceiling. Sumptuous furs and velvet throws cover an enormous round bed. In the center of the room, a fountain plays in a shallow pool. Five jewel-encrusted bottles sit on a shelf near the bed. Massage oils, warming lotions, lube. A box of condoms. The chest on the floor holds dildos, vibrators, butt plugs, and various other toys in sealed packaging. I lower the lid, almost toppling the lamp from the adjacent nightstand. I've never been so nervous in my life. After another circuit of the room, I sit down and wipe my sweaty palms on the embroidered covering of the chaise.

From my seat, I have a clear view of the door. Soft classical music drifts through the room from hidden speakers. After an eternity, there's a knock, the click of a lock, and a slice of light as the door swings open. The moisture leaves my mouth. Broad shoulders fill the opening. I swallow hard, pressing a hand against my stomach to quiet the butterflies inside. It's him. Looking taller, sexier, and oh-so mysterious with the mask covering his eyes. He scans the dimly lit room, catches sight of me, and strides in my direction.

"I was afraid you wouldn't come." His voice is deeper than I remember, rougher. The devastation of the day disappears. In its place, a thrill of anticipation forms in the pit of my belly. He's back, and he's here for me. I can't wait to hear that sexy baritone whisper naughty things in my ears.

"I was about to leave." An ache begins to blossom between my legs, brought about by the promise of illicit, non-committal sex. I press my thighs together, hoping he won't notice the way my hands shake as I lift my wine glass to my lips. The liquid sloshes up to the rim, almost but not quite spilling over. Goodness, he's delicious, dressed in black from head to toe. Tuxedos were made for men like him, men with broad chests, slim hips, and devilish grins.

"Have you changed your mind?" He pauses a few feet from me. "Do you want to call it off?"

I tilt my head up to catch a better glimpse of his face, his square jaw, the curve of his lips. "No, it's just— I'm not sure what I'm doing here." The air in the room thickens, making it difficult to breathe, and it's his fault. His maleness is over-whelming.

"If you're here, it's because you know I can give you something no one else can." Those are cryptic words coming from a man with no face, no identity, and no name. "Isn't that right?"

"I— Uh— I'm not sure." My heart thunders like a jackrabbit until the sound of rushing blood in my ears replaces the splash of water from the fountain. "I think so."

"Relax. We don't have to do anything. We can talk if you'd like." One of his hands removes the wine glass from my grasp and places it on the table at my side. His fingers slide through mine, pulling me to my feet until the tips of my breasts hover a millimeter away from his chest. God, I can feel the heat radiating off of him, through the thin satin of my gown and into my skin. His warmth pulls me to him, enveloping me, chasing away the chill of the unknown. "Or you can leave. The choice is yours. Anything that happens in this room is with your consent."

"No. I'll stay." The declaration flies from my lips, sneaking past my common sense. This is crazy. The words repeat over and over in my head, unheeded. I don't run. Instead, I cling to his hand, enjoying the glide of his skin against mine. There's so much power in his touch. It tingles along my skin, sizzling across my nerve endings, exciting every synapse.

"Why did you come here tonight?" From behind his mask, his light eyes bore into me, searching out my secrets. "Tell me."

"Isn't it obvious?" I place my palms on his chest and slide my hands up the front of his shirt. He's as hard and lean as I remember, a wall of muscle wrapped in silk and linen. "I'm curious about you."

"But that's not the only reason."

"I've had an awful year." I close my eyes to blot out visions of my ex-husband with his assistant and their new baby, Nicky with the starlet, my father with Lavender. So many men. So many betrayals. When I open my eyes, he's staring down at me. I moisten my lips to speak. The most important men in my life underestimated my value, a mistake I won't let happen again. "I just need to forget about my life for a little while."

"Fair enough." With the back of a finger, he strokes the side of my face. The light touch tingles in my breasts and thighs. "I might have been mistaken about you."

"What do you mean?"

"I thought you were a good girl, but you're not. Good girls don't show up at sex clubs to fuck a total stranger, do they?"

"No." The dampness between my legs increases with every caress. His hand skates along the column of my throat, tickles along my collarbone. I like his chastising words, the heat in his gaze behind the mask, the hitch in his breath when I touch him. "I'm not a good girl."

"Good girls don't wear dresses like this, do they? No bra, and I bet no panties either. Look at your hard nipples staring at me, your dress so tight I can see the outline of your pussy." His gaze peruses my body, weighted down by lust. My gown is a luminescent blue that brings out the color of my eyes. The satin clings to every nuance of my figure. I would never wear something so trashy in public, but rules are made to be broken at the Devil's Playground. He tweaks a nipple through the fabric, sending ripples of delight into my core. "Did you wear this dress for me?"

No man has ever spoken to me this way. I'm confused and excited and—and grateful. "Yes. Do you like it?"

"I love it. You're the most beautiful creature I've ever seen. You have a body made for fucking and a mouth made for sucking. I can't wait to shove my dick inside you, fill you up with my cum, make you scream my name. Do you want me to do that to you? Is that what you want from me tonight?"

"Yes." God, yes. My lungs swell and contract, desperate for more oxygen, because this man has stolen all the air from my world. The scent of his cologne drifts in his wake as he circles me, inspecting me from head to toe. Under his scrutiny, my breasts grow heavier; the tips prickle with arousal. I clench my knees together, looking for relief from the dull ache in my pussy. If he doesn't fuck me soon, I'm going to implode.

"Aren't you curious? About what I want from you? Worried even?"

"A little." Although my shoes have ridiculously high heels, he's still taller than me, a rarity for a five-eight woman. I turn my face up to his, admiring the sharp planes of his cheekbones and the glints of auburn, brown, and gold in his goatee. How will those whiskers feel on the soft flesh of my belly or between my legs? I already know the answer. Fucking awesome.

The right corner of his mouth tips upward. He places a finger beneath my chin, angles my head up, and lowers his nose until his lips are so, so close. Close enough to feel his breath, to smell hints of bourbon. "I want to control you. To guide your desires. To make you want things you never knew you wanted. Make you do things you never thought you could do. I want you to beg for mercy and forgiveness. All while I use your body to pleasure my own." Slowly, his mouth creeps to my ear. He takes my earlobe between his teeth and tugs. I feel the pull in my pussy. "And when I'm done with you, you're going to thank me for all the orgasms I gave you."

Holy shitballs. I'm breathing hard, like I ran a footrace. How does he know my darkest, dirtiest fantasies? Things I've never admitted to myself, let alone a perfect stranger. We stare at each other, enveloped in secrets and mystery. I have no idea who he is. I don't care, but I have to ask. "You tracked me down. You know my name. If Roman finds out you breached his NDA, he'll have our heads."

"Roman isn't going to find out unless you tell him." The sweep of his touch along my arms to my hips echoes the path of his gaze. By the time his eyes find mine again, every inch of my body is on edge.

"It's not fair. I have no idea who you are." The anonymity excites me. He could be anyone—a gangster, a politician, maybe even the prince we saw on the street today. "Are you Prince Henry?" His lips part like he's going to speak. I press a fingertip against them to silence his words. "No. On second thought, don't tell me." If I don't know his name, I won't have to obsess about meeting his expectations or seeing him with another woman. The notion is liberating.

"Inside this room, our names make no difference." The caress of his hands along my arms escalates my pulse. "Can you live with that?"

"Yes." The solitary word is breathy, desperate. I don't care if he's the King of Siam. I just need his hands on me.

"Touch yourself. Show me how much you want this."

I float a palm over one breast. The tip of my nipple pokes my hand, sharp as a pin beneath the satin. A groan of approval rumbles from his chest. "Are we really doing this?" I'm tied up in knots inside. My body wants to fuck. My head is screaming that I'm insane. "This doesn't seem real."

"I'm flesh and blood, madam." Wrapping his fingers around my wrists, he places my hands on his hard, hotter-than-the-flames-of-hell chest. His ribs rise and fall with each breath. The strong surge of his heart thumps against my palm. My skin pebbles as his hands slide down the bare skin revealed by the cutout in the back of my dress, slowing to cup my ass.

"You're so warm." Standing close to him, having his hands on me, releases my inhibitions. Reason goes out the door when my fingers find the lapels of his jacket. I remove his tie, open the collar of his shirt, and unbutton the front to reveal ripple after ripple of abs, pecs, and a dusting of dark blond, wiry hair.

He runs the tip of his tongue over his lower lip. "Are we going to fuck now, gorgeous?" The way he speaks those filthy words in his posh accent increases the wetness between my legs.

"If we don't, I'm going to be really disappointed."

My confession snaps the fragile thread of restraint stretched between us. He picks me up by the waist, pushing me into the wall behind us, crashing me into the paneling. I wrap a leg around his hip and grind against the steel rod inside his trousers. A primeval growl rumbles from his lips.

JEANA E MANN

Hot, wet kisses trail down the column of my neck. I dig my fingers into his short hair. Fuck Nicky. Fuck my ex-husband. Fuck me. This is by far the most exciting thing that has ever happened to me, and I'm going to enjoy every single, sinful, scandalous moment.

"I take it things didn't work out between you and your wank of a boyfriend." He slips the straps of my gown over my shoulders, baring me to the waist, trapping my arms with the delicate fabric. The breath behind his words burns against my collarbone.

"He's history."

"Are you angry with him?" He bends at the knees to trail kisses down my sternum to my breast. Each press of his lips brands me, burns through my skin, ruining me. He sucks an eager nipple into his mouth.

I throw my head back and moan. "I'm angry at all men in general," I manage to confess, unable to think of anything but having him inside me.

"Excellent. Let's see if we can fuck that out of you tonight."

In one lightning-fast motion, he spins me around, bends me over, and shoves my face into the bed. Something soft binds my wrists behind my back. I'm too shocked to make a sound. Cool air wafts over my bare skin as he bunches my dress around my waist. One of his legs kicks my feet apart. I'm open to him, pussy on full display, ass in the air.

"Look how wet you are. You want my cock, don't you?" He runs a finger up the wetness dripping along the inside of my thigh then slides a finger between the folds of my pussy. "Do you like it rough, my sweet?"

"Yes." I try to buck against his hand, but he holds me down with a palm against the small of my back. "Please."

"Do you have a safe word?"

"No." My inner muscles flutter in a pre-orgasmic warning.

"For tonight, your safe word is Lancelot." A rustle of fabric accompanies his declaration. I think he's undressing further, but I can't see with my face in the mattress.

"Do I need a safe word?"

"Absolutely." He tugs on the restraint around my wrists, testing the knot. "This is our first time, and I want to test your boundaries."

Excitement barrels through me. He's barely touched me, but I'm ready to come. The truth punches me in the gut. At this moment, I'm willing to fuck any man who gets inside my panties. Except I'm not wearing any. Proving my theory. Tears leak from the corners of my eyes, making dark, wet circles on the velvet bedspread. "I don't have any boundaries. I'm a slut."

A sharp slap stings across my right butt cheek. He grabs the hair at my nape, twisting my head around to face him, his grip firm but gentle. "Don't ever say that." With the backs of his fingers, he gently wipes the wetness from my cheeks. Bending down, he brushes his lips along the shell of my ear and whispers, "Knowing what you want in bed and asking for it is never wrong. Do you understand?"

Emotions bubble up from nowhere. Shame. Excitement. Curiosity. Desire. I nod, my throat too raw for speech. Until now, I've always been told how to think—by my parents and society, my teachers, friends, lovers. But inside these four walls, I'm free to be whomever I please. To do whatever I want. The knot of anxiety in my gut untangles. I blow out a cleansing breath, feeling lighter than I've felt in weeks.

The golden stranger caresses my cheek one last time. "Excellent. Are you ready?"

"Yes." My voice breaks, like I haven't spoken in hours. Fear heightens my arousal. It creeps along my skin, rising in gooseflesh, and settles in the deepest recesses of my body, eager for more of him.

A cocky smile reveals his even white teeth. Over my shoulder, I watch as he shrugs out of his jacket, staring down at me behind a veil of anonymity. With a snap, he frees the black bowtie from his collar and stuffs it between my lips. "Then let's begin."

8

HENRY

"*Y*our Highness? Prince Heinrich?" From far away, I hear a female voice.

"Pardon?" My collar suddenly seems too tight. I run a finger around the inside perimeter to ease the constriction. The faces of my staff stare at me.

Since last night, I've been unable to think of anything or anyone but Everly. The tightness of her cunt around my cock. The way her pussy clamped down on my fingers when I made her come. I've never been with any woman so responsive, so thirsty for domination, in my entire life. Beneath the conference table, my dick swells, pushing against the fly of my trousers.

"Sir, are you okay?"

"I'm fine." Except for a lingering sexual hangover. "Shasta, did you take care of the contracts I spoke with you about this morning?" A thrill of anticipation skates down my back.

Once Everly signs the appropriate paperwork, I can look forward to many more nights between her legs.

"Yes, sir." Shasta's glasses slip down her nose. She pushes them into place with an index finger. "The Magnussons have issued an invitation to their son's wedding in September. Will you be attending?"

"No. Send my regrets." Sven Magnusson has been trying to fix me up with his vapid daughter since she reached puberty. At some point, I'll have to choose a wife, but not yet. And certainly not her. Right now, I can't think of anyone but Everly.

"What about the ribbon-cutting ceremony in Monaco?"

I shake my head, glance at my watch, and sigh as Shasta rolls through a dozen more invitations. Meanwhile, everything reminds me of Everly. The color of the sky outside is the same hue as her eyes. The round shapes of the apples in the fruit basket mimic the swell of her breasts. God, those tits. Her nipples were pale pink, incredibly sensitive, and became hard nubs when I sucked them into my mouth. With a little work, I could probably train her to orgasm from nipple play alone.

"You have dinner reservations tonight with the governor of New York and his wife. They want to know if you have any special requests."

"No." Underneath the table, my dick pulses. The ache in my balls is unbearable. "Can you all step out, please? I need a minute."

"Certainly, Your Highness." Shasta grabs her phone and tablet from the table. The rest of the staff rises, shoving their chairs aside, and make a quick exit.

As soon as the door closes behind the last person, I step into the bathroom, lock the door, and unzip. My cock springs forward the second I pull down my boxers. A bead of moisture glistens on the tip. I wrap my fingers around the base and stroke to the crown. Jesus. If my balls get any tighter, they're going to burst. On the second stroke, I remember Everly's pleas to have me inside her. The way I pounded into her, thrusting and grunting, lost in the sounds of our slapping skin, surrounded by the scent of her arousal. The third stroke conjures up memories of her on her knees, my cock in her mouth, hands tied behind her back, the little choking noises she made when I hit the back of her throat.

My balls draw up, tighter than I ever thought possible. Hot fire races through my veins, spurred by the need to release the tension. I'm a little sore from all the late-night fucking, but I don't stop pumping my fist. Harder and faster. Precise and measured at first. Sloppy at the last. The same way I fucked her. My thoughts muddy and collide with images of her alabaster skin, nips and slaps, clutching fingers, and the vise grip of her silky thighs around my waist.

"Fuck." The word rips from my throat, the growl of a beast. I place a hand on the wall above the toilet, giving in to the frenzied pump of my hand, fucking my fingers like a sex-starved freak. My bicep aches. My lungs burn. I squeeze my shaft, throw back my head, and roar. Hot ejaculate spurts over my fist. Relief chases my orgasm and washes through my body from head to toe.

I ride out the wave of pleasure until my heartbeat starts to calm. My reflection in the mirror shows a wild-eyed brute of a man with the flush of guilt on his face and a secret smirk on his lips. I clean myself up, splash water on my face, and take a minute to get my head together. Now that the flush of orgasm has faded, I'm as unsettled as before. How can that be? It was just a night of shagging, and she's just a girl.

Even as I think the words, I know it's a lie. She's not just anyone. She's Don McElroy's only child and the best sex I've ever had. She did everything I asked and more. She gave all of herself to a complete stranger, without question, willingly, looking like a goddess the entire time. My traitorous dick stirs at the memory.

A knock on the door interrupts my musings. I jump. Shasta's muffled voice comes from the other side. "Excuse me, sir? I apologize for the interruption. There's a Mr. Tarnovsky here to see you. Shall I send him away? He says it's urgent."

"No. It's fine. Send him to the living room. I'll be there in a minute." Following the second splash of cold water on my face, I straighten my clothing, put on my best scowl, and prepare for Nikolay's impudence.

"Your Royal Highness, I apologize for the impromptu visit. Thank you for taking time out of your hectic schedule to meet with me." He bows, a pleasant smile on his face. "Roman sends his regards." For a brief second, I'm reminded of the old Nicky. The one who shared my dorm room, my best friend, my mate for pub crawls and polo matches. I've missed him. If this were a different world, if he hadn't betrayed me, I'd be happy to see him.

"Good morning." To my surprise, it isn't the memory of my ex-fiancée in his bed that haunts me as much as the picture of him with Everly. His fingers on her porcelain flesh. Their shared smiles. His possessive hand on her back. Now that I know just how special she is, with the feel of her fresh on my cock, I begrudge every finger he ever laid upon her. "Have a seat." I gesture toward the sofa.

He pauses at the mirror over the credenza to tweak the knot in his tie. Always preening. Always cocky. "After the way you snubbed me at the Devil's Playground last time, I thought maybe you were still mad at me over Kitty Cat."

I remember every detail of that night. My girlfriend. My bed. My devastation. The ache of my fist after I punched him in the jaw. The only thing minimizing my anger is the way I debauched his ex-girlfriend last night, made her lick my feet, and jack me off. A triumphant smile stretches my face. "You never apologized. Is that why you're here? Did you finally grow a conscience?"

His sigh is audible. "I admit that my behavior was less than admirable." He lounges on the sofa, an arm thrown across the back, crossing an ankle over his knee. I claim the chair across from him, sitting a bit higher so he has to look up at me. Little things like this matter. It's a subtle clue that he's on my territory, that I'm the one in control. Power means everything to people like us. "But that was years ago. I'm a different man." He waves to the butler. "Do you think I could get a drink?"

"It's okay, Mr. Hobson. My guest isn't staying." I gesture for the man to leave the room and turn back to Nicky. "Say what you need and get out."

Nicky rolls his eyes before picking up the previous conversation. "You didn't really love Kitty, did you? I mean, *really* love her? After all, she was always such a bitch. And you moved on, right? You never seem to be short of women at your side. I've seen the pictures of you on your yacht with all those babes in bikinis. Weren't you linked to some model? What was her name? Tanya? Tamara?"

"Tatyana." The first time I wrapped my fingers around her throat during sex, she'd locked herself in the bathroom and cried for an hour. Needless to say, our breakup had been less than amicable. "And yes, I was in love with Catherine. You knew that, yet you screwed her anyway." At the time, it felt like someone had ripped my beating heart out of my chest and tossed into a pit of flaming coals. That was the first, last, and only time I risked my affections on a woman and the end of my friendship with Nikolay Reznik Tarnovsky. "What kind of friend does that?"

"I did you a favor, and you know it. She shagged half the rugby team behind your back." He rests a hand on his thigh, drumming his fingers like he's impatient to move forward. So am I. Reliving past mistakes only makes a person bitter. I need to move on.

"Maybe." Kitty had hidden her dark side from me. If I hadn't caught them together, I might never have known what a lying, deceitful bitch she was. The trajectory of my life would've been much different and much more miserable. Leave it to Nick to turn an unpardonable act into a gift.

"Fine." He throws a hand up in the air. "I apologize. I'm a horrible person, and it was a rotten thing to do."

I stare at him, contemplating his sincerity. He's too intelligent to be trusted. "Is this your 'emergency'?" I draw air quotes around the last word. "Did you wake up this morning overcome with guilt? Forgive me if I can't swallow the sudden change in your personality."

"No, I'm here on business, actually." He smooths the placket of his shirt, something he does when he's nervous. The gesture pleases me. It means I've gained the upper hand in the conversation. "Roman sent me."

"Really?" I shift to the edge of the chair, unbuttoning my jacket to lean forward. "Go on."

"Let's discuss it over lunch." The fabric of his jacket parts to reveal a pin-striped vest. "I can brief you."

No matter my feelings about him, the opportunity to lessen Androvia's problems is paramount. "Let me notify my security team of the change in schedule."

While I text Shasta to deal with the logistics, Nick goes to the window. With his back to me, he stares down at the street. I don't trust him. His cocky attitude, sketchy business deals, and cavalier disregard for other people have made him a despised member of the underground. Roman's protection is the only thing standing between him and an unmarked grave in the middle of some desert. I almost feel sorry for him.

"There's a storm brewing," he says, his voice softer than usual, lifting the hairs on the back of my neck. Outside the window, fluffy white clouds drift lazily in a brilliant blue sky. I have a feeling he's right.

9

HENRY

*F*ormer Vice President Don McElroy greets us in the lobby of the Chelsea restaurant. Now that I know he's Everly's father, I can see the resemblance. They're both tall and fair-skinned and confident in their movements. I cast a questioning glance at Nicky, stunned into silence. Lunch with the enemy wasn't on my agenda.

"Don, hello." Nicky ignores my scowl and steps forward. They shake hands and slap each other on the back, like old friends. "I hope we didn't keep you waiting too long."

"Not at all. It's good to see you. You too, Prince Heinrich. Glad you could make it." Like Everly, Don McElroy is long-limbed and fair-skinned. Threads of dark auburn weave through his silver hair.

I lift an eyebrow at Nicky. As much as I'd like to abandon this ambush, my curiosity is piqued. "I didn't know you were joining us."

"Did I forget to mention Don would be here? My apologies." Nick feigns embarrassment, but I know better. The canny motherfucker planned this all along. Another excellent example of his untrustworthiness.

Don's blue eyes rove over me. "I hope it's not a problem." He bows and waits for me to extend a hand to shake, following royal protocol. I don't want to touch this bastard, but a lifetime of training kicks in. His palm is smooth, his grip firm. "The last time we met, you were a lad of fourteen and twelve inches shorter."

I have faint memories of him, solid and congenial, at my father's coronation, his name mentioned in after-dinner conversations at the palace, and photographs of his arm around the king on royal hunting expeditions. When I was a kid, he seemed like the epitome of the American male. The wisdom of experience allows me to see beyond his orchestrated smiles, firm handshakes, and the hollow promises reeking of a politician's insincerity. Sometimes the most dangerous men lurk behind the façade of a hero. I should know. My family tree is full of them.

"Please give your mother my best regards. She was on holiday in Spain the last time Judy and I visited. And your father? How's he doing?" His voice booms with quiet authority in the five-star Chelsea restaurant.

"They're both well. Thank you for asking." Although we're in the middle of a crowded establishment, the threat of danger prickles my skin. I mustn't let down my guard, not for a second. A quick glance around the room eases my anxiety. My security team is stationed around the perimeter and outside the restaurant, steps away from my side.

"Well, I'm glad to hear it." His gaze flickers across my face, assessing and unconvinced. The game of power has begun. I'm lying. He knows it. My father's mental health has been a subject of hot debate among his subjects and journalists for the past year. We fall silent as the hostess approaches.

"Vice President McElroy. Your Royal Highness. Nicky."
She's thin and short, with dark red lipstick. The smile on her
face widens when it lands on the traitorous Russian. The
grin he flashes her is equal parts of sin and invitation. She
bats her long eyelashes in silent flirtation before stepping
into the dining area. "Gentlemen, if you'll follow me, your
table is this way."

Expansive windows offer a view of the Hudson River.
Sailboats glide through the water, enjoying the sunny afternoon. Halfway to our table, surprise leaves my throat dry.
There's no mistaking the shine of long red hair or the softness of perfect, alabaster skin. It's her. Everly. I cast a glance
at Nick. He drags a palm over his tie, fighting a frown. His
gaze catches mine then flicks away. What's that about? Guilt?
Annoyance?

"My daughter's here. Let's stop and say hello." McElroy
shifts direction.

The blonde seated with Everly seems familiar, but my
gaze is locked on my dream girl. An attractive blush climbs
up her elegant neck before settling in her cheeks. I wait for
recognition to flicker in her eyes, but it never appears. My
focus homes in on her lips. That same pouty mouth did
filthy, exquisite things to my body last night. Blood rockets
to my groin, awakening my cock, ready for a replay.

"Rourke, a pleasure, as always." McElroy places a hand on
her shoulder. Displeasure flashes across her face so quickly I
wonder if I imagined it. An intriguing tension thickens
between Everly, Rourke, Don, and Nicky. "Let me introduce
you to my colleagues. Prince Heinrich, this is Rourke
Menshikov. Rourke, meet the Crown Prince of Androvia.
And you know Nicky, of course." Roman's wife nods and
smiles. I take her hand and make the appropriate remarks,
unable to rip my attention from Everly. "And this is my
daughter, Everly."

"Ah, yes, the delightful Ms. McElroy. I've heard so much about you." With her hand in mine, I bend to place a kiss on her fingertips. At the touch of her skin to my mouth, a tingle buzzes over my lips. I pile on the charisma, knowing Nicky is listening to every word, eager to annoy him. "You're even lovelier than your reputation." My gaze locks on hers. I wait for a glimmer of recognition that doesn't arrive.

Everly flashes her mega-watt smile. "What brings you to New York, Prince Heinrich? I'm disappointed our paths haven't crossed sooner." A hint of flirtation hovers behind her words.

My pulse quickens at the low, smooth sound of her voice, remembering her pleas for mercy, begging me to make her come. "Business with your father brought me into the city, but I have a house here, as well. Two, actually." I sound like an arrogant ass, overeager to impress her. The truth is I haven't visited either house in the past year, preferring the bustle of a downtown hotel to the solitude of my large, echoing, lonely homes. To redeem myself, I make another stupid comment. Her smile widens, and I'm gone. Gone for her loveliness and charm and the way my nerve endings come alive at her touch. The rest of the conversation blurs into the background. I'm too taken by the subtle hint of hatred in her eyes whenever she glances at Nick. Good. Let her hate him.

Seeing her in the light of day cements my resolve. I need this woman in my life. Not only will she satisfy my sexual desires, but she'll also provide a link to her father, a way to keep tabs on his actions. My mind is made up. The only thing left is to convince her. And that means revealing my identity.

EVERLY

No matter how hard I try, I can't keep my eyes off the handsome prince seated with my father. His blue eyes meet mine with a force that takes my breath away. My heartbeat stalls. The corner of his mouth curls into a wicked grin. My pulse starts up again, doubling its pace until spots form in front of my eyes.

Across the room, my father joins the prince in staring at me, but his gaze is filled with warning. I lift my chin in direct defiance. The prince's grin dissipates into something more serious, almost cunning, tugging on something low in my belly. That shrewd expression confirms my suspicions. The prince is the one who spanked my ass until it glowed red then made me come harder than I've ever done in my life. I glance away, feeling a rising tide of embarrassment in my cheeks.

Nicky takes my hand in his. I keep forgetting about him. His touch annoys me. If only he'd go back to his table. He squeezes my fingers to draw my attention. "I want to apologize for my behavior toward you. It was inexcusable." My jaw drops in shock. An apology was the last thing I expected. I don't have time for this. Not now. "I mistreated you, and I'm ashamed. If I led you on, I'm sorry. I hope you won't see my actions as a reflection on your value as a person. You're kind, beautiful, and deserve much more than I could ever give. We both know I'm not the sort of man you want in your life. I hope we can start over and be friends."

"I—I—don't know what to say." I glance at Rourke. I want to believe him, but I suspect this is a show for her approval.

She shakes her head, echoing my disbelief. The prince's introspection morphs into a scowl. I don't know if it's something my father said to him or the way Nicky is down on one knee in front of me, but he's definitely annoyed.

"We're going to run into each other from time to time. I don't want you to be uncomfortable because I'm a dick. Say you forgive me, and let's move on." Nicky flashes his most charming smile at me, but his gaze is on Rourke. Although I love her more than the world, I can't stop the resentment slicing through my chest. He's in love with her. It's so obvious. I'm always losing out to someone else. A Hollywood starlet. Or, in the case of my ex-husband, his employee. And then I hate myself for allowing such destructive thoughts to enter my head.

"I can live with that." As much as I want to continue hating him, I need to focus on the future and repairing my life. Things I can't accomplish beneath the chains of hurt and anger.

Nicky and Rourke resume their conversation, but I can't concentrate on their words. I'm too enamored with the golden-haired man across the room. Does he know I know? Should I say something or keep quiet? Our night together was meant to be an isolated incident. Watching him now brings back all the excitement of his touch. I press my thighs together to stave off the growing ache. My golden stranger is a prince.

10

HENRY

*a*cross the restaurant, I peer over the menu in my hand as Nicky speaks to Everly. She doesn't look directly at him. From my seat, I have a clear view of her long legs beneath the table. Legs that were wrapped around my waist a short time ago. Legs that twitched before she came so hard on my dick, it drove me to orgasm.

"How is Androvia's economy?" Don tries to draw my attention away from his daughter, but I can't concentrate. I'm jealous of her knit dress, the way it clings to the swells of her breasts, caressing skin that I know from experience is soft and smooth and creamy. "The last I heard, unemployment was up."

"About the same, I believe." Reluctantly, I tear my gaze from Everly to focus on my host. "I have a few ideas to bolster growth." Over the past year, my proposals had passed through Androvian Parliament but had been denied by my father. Unless a plan directly fattens his purse, he has no interest.

"It's good to see you take an interest in your people." He rubs his chin and nods. "Have you thought about the political stance you'll take when you become king? Your father isn't getting any younger. You need to be prepared for the unexpected." Don's blue eyes bore into mine. An ominous foreboding rouses the tiny hairs on the back of my neck. Menace lurks behind his relaxed demeanor. "If he should suddenly drop dead, you should have a plan in place."

"That's an odd thing to say. Do you know something I don't?" On instinct, I shutter my expression. Across the room, Nicky has Everly's hand in his. A silent growl rumbles in my throat. She might have been his in the beginning, but she's mine now. "Androvia's in a tough spot, especially with its throne in jeopardy."

"You're mistaken. There's no threat to the crown." My attention bounces between McElroy and his daughter. The waiter presents a bottle of wine for our approval and fills our glasses. Meanwhile, Nicky takes a knee in front of Everly. What the ever-loving fuck? Is he proposing? My fingers clench around the napkin in my lap. Don's gaze follows mine.

"She's beautiful, isn't she? Just like her mother." A cunning smile curls his lips. Although the room is spacious, the walls close in around me. "They look great together. If I have my way, Nicky will be my next son-in-law."

"You mean a cheating, deceitful son-in-law. I thought a man like you would have higher goals for his daughter." I swallow, forcing myself to once again look away from his daughter and my former best mate. I don't like Nicky touching her. Not after I branded her. Not with the memory of her wet heat fresh in my mind. "No woman deserves that."

"He's a pretentious asshole, but his connections to Roman make him highly desirable. Imagine the power of a union like theirs." Don stares out the window at the shimmering river. "You, of all people, should understand the necessity of building alliances through marriage." I've seen that dreamy look before on my father's face when he was drunk on visions of domination and revenge. "Not that I'm a fan of Roman, by any means. He's getting too big for his britches, in my opinion."

"And what about Everly? Maybe she doesn't want to be married to a pretentious asshole."

"She'll do whatever I tell her to do." He taps a thoughtful fingernail on the edge of his wineglass. "I had high hopes for her, but she's turned out to be more of a hinderance than an asset. I can only hope she'll marry up this next time."

"I'd hardly call Nick marrying up." I understand his school of thought. In our world, connections are everything. Marriages are brokered like business deals. Love is a foolish notion for paupers and romance novels. I should know. My parents have been trotting eligible females in front of me since my fifth birthday. I draw in a deep breath through my nose to clear my head. What do I care? Everly was a one-night stand. Nothing more. The sooner I accept the fact, the better.

"My wife and I had hoped for a boy, but nature doesn't always grant our wishes. Take my advice. Start working on a male heir right away, before time gets away from you. Do you still have an arrangement with Lady Clayton? I was the one who suggested your union, you know. Back when your father actually listened to my advice." His gaze cuts through me. "She'll make a fantastic queen."

I choke on a sip of wine. The arrangement was a stupid concession on my part, made when I was too young to know better. Our engagement is off, but she's still the number one contender for my queen. After all, it doesn't really matter who I wed as long as she's of royal blood, useful to the throne, and able to bear children. I clear my throat and try not to grimace at the thought of marriage to a two-faced bitch. I have plenty of time to find someone else. "Anything you've heard about a marriage between us is sheer speculation."

"Is it?" One of his thick gray eyebrows arches toward his hairline. "I have it on good authority that Lord Clayton paid a handsome sum to your parents as confirmation."

"You certainly know a lot about my situation. Why is that?"

"Your father and I used to be very close. In fact, there was a time when I considered a match between you and my daughter." His lips purse while he swirls the wine in his glass until it spins hypnotically.

Heat races up my neck. The idea of owning Everly, having her at my disposal night and day, is a heady but unrealistic one. "She's not a royal."

"Not technically, but did you know my wife is a cousin to the Queen of England?" Don mistakes my silence as interest and continues. "She gave up her title to marry me and become a U.S. citizen." He taps a finger on the corner of his placemat then leans closer, like he's going to reveal a secret. "Look at her. She's beautiful, smart, fertile." My gaze flicks to Everly's long legs. "I'd be willing to sell her to you. Name your price."

What kind of father speaks that way about his daughter? Frustration on her behalf tightens the muscles in my chest. He has to love and protect her, not sell her off to the highest bidder. I take a sip of water and choose my next words carefully. "I don't need to buy a wife. If I wanted your daughter, I'd just take her."

What the devil is taking Nicky so long? I blame him for putting me in this situation with McElroy. He's having a heated conversation with Mrs. Menshikov, taking his damn time returning to our table. Everly shifts in her seat, appearing uncomfortable with the confrontation in front of her. Our gazes lock once more, resurrecting that strange, exciting twitter in my gut.

Don's complexion deepens to dark red. "Don't let your ego get in the way of your common sense, Your Highness. No one takes anything from me unless I let them. Just ask Roman. He tried to fuck with my business, and now he's under suspicion for murder. Coincidence? I'll let you decide." He throws a casual arm across Nicky's empty chair.

"You seem to have things all figured out." In an echo of his nonchalance, I lean back in my chair. The back of my neck prickles under the threat of danger to myself, my country, and Everly. "Maybe you're the one who needs to check his ego at the door."

"Don't underestimate the scope of my connections. If you're going to be the next king—"

My temper begins to flare. "You mean *when—when* I become king."

"*If* you become king, you need to line up your allies right away. Get a strong team behind you. All I ask is for Androvia to provide refuge and support to my business partners." With a graceful flick of his fingers, he releases the buttons of his jacket and shoves back in his chair. "Your father has outlived his usefulness to my supporters and me. Thankfully, you seem to be much more intelligent than him. Do the right thing, Your Highness. I can help you make Androvia great again."

His veiled threats heighten my discomfort. The possibility that I might not make it to the throne has never occurred to me. I'm the sole male heir of the current monarch. My uncle Rupert, whose political inclinations align with Father's, would be next in succession. "I don't know which is more disturbing—the offer to sell your daughter or your inappropriate interest in my country."

"I have interests around the world, Your Highness. Your father has been most generous in his support over the past decade, but lately, he's been less than accommodating to the needs of my associates. That kind of negligence could separate a person's head from his neck." The gleam in his blue eyes reminds me of glacier ice.

"I'm done with this conversation." I nod to my closest bodyguard, a silent signal to pull the limo around to the front.

"Just stating the facts, son." He nods to the waiter for a refill of his wineglass, oblivious to my growing irritation.

"I'm not your son. I'm the Crown Prince of Androvia, and it would be in your best interest to remember it." My shoulders tense at his intentional insults. If he's trying to get under my skin, he's doing an excellent job.

"I beg your pardon. I meant no affront." He lifts a hand. "It's just that my partners and I would like to see someone new in charge of Androvia, someone like yourself. Someone young and with vision. Someone amenable to change."

"Talk of a coup is treason. I have many faults, but disloyalty has never been one of them." As much as I dislike my father, I have no plans to overthrow his claim to the throne. Not when I can achieve the same result through patience and proper planning. "If I were you, I'd choose my next words very carefully."

"I know this is a hard conversation, but you need to be ready. These people have made your father a wealthy man. They can do the same for you."

My net worth is triple that of my father's. I can afford to be self-righteous. Unlike King Gustav, money matters less to me than the good fortunes of the people in my kingdom. "I'm not interested."

"Don't be a fool, Your Highness."

"That's the last time you'll insult me." The muscles in my jaw tense until they ache. "In my opinion, you're the reason my country is in such a mess."

"What did I miss?" Nicky returns, sliding into his chair.

"Veiled threats. Subterfuge. All served with a healthy dose of treason," I reply.

"Sounds fascinating." Nicky waggles his eyebrows. "Count me in."

The waiter approaches to take our orders. My appetite has evaporated, along with my patience. While Don and Nick recite their choices off the menu, I watch Everly's face. Her gaze meets mine, flicks away, then returns. A pleasant tickle teases my lower belly. She bites her lower lip with even white teeth. The corners of her mouth curl upward. A dozen yards separate us, but for the space of a heartbeat, we're the only ones in the room.

Nicky keeps his gaze trained on my face. Curiosity flashes across his expression. "Catch me up."

"I was just trying to persuade Prince Henry to consider the advantages of my counsel." Arrogance oozes from Don. He's so smug, so damn self-righteous. My dislike for him grows with each passing second.

"And how did he take the offer?" Nicky lifts an eyebrow.

"He thinks both of you should fuck off." My blood pressure climbs until it sings through my ears. *Stay calm, Henry.* I toss my napkin onto the table.

"You're a cocky bastard." Don's lips flatten into a sneer. So much for the venerated humanitarian and hero. "That's dangerous talk."

I lower my voice, forcing a neutral expression. "Like you, I have many powerful friends. And I can guarantee they don't give two fucks about you or your agenda."

"Whoa. Gentlemen." Nicky raises both palms into the air.

"I leave you alone for a minute, and you're ready to declare war against each other."

"Whatever it takes," Don says.

"You're messing with the wrong man." I signal to the waiter for the check. I'm done. "I'm not my father. You can't buy me."

"Every man has his price."

"Not me," I reply.

Across the room, Rourke Menshikov leaves the restaurant. Everly sits alone. Seconds later, she heads in the direction of the ladies' room. Don follows her.

"You set me up." I turn to Nicky, my temper barely restrained.

He shrugs and dabs the corners of his lips with his napkin. "It was necessary. Roman needed to distract Don for a few hours, and this was the only way I could get him away from his office."

"You could've just told me."

"Maybe. But this was so much more fun."

I leave Nicky alone at the table and head for the door. Fuck him. Fuck McElroy. No one threatens my country and gets away with it. As I stride across the dining room, Everly barrels through the exit door. I follow on her heels. Don McElroy needs a reality check, and I know just how to get his attention.

 VERLY

INSIDE THE RESTAURANT BATHROOM, I brace my hands against the sink. I'm not sure where the conversation with Rourke turned sour, but it did—in a big way. She raced out of the building, leaving me stunned and hurt. The bathroom attendant lowers her eyes when my gaze meets hers in the mirror. I can't blame Rourke for being upset. She's newly pregnant, and Roman is the lead suspect in Lavender Cunningham's murder. I should have told her about my father's affair with the party planner, but I couldn't bring myself to betray the most important man in my life. Airing the McElroy family dirty laundry would only complicate the situation. To calm my racing heart, I switch on the tap. The water flows over my wrists, chilling my hot skin. Rourke, my father, Nicky, Prince Heinrich—they're the stars in my living nightmare. One I'm eager to escape.

New-age music pipes into the elegant restroom through

hidden speakers. The flute and piano duet screeches in my head like nails on a chalkboard. The walls close in around me. I grab my purse and dash out the door. In the narrow corridor, two strong hands clamp around my upper arms.

"One minute, young lady." Father's authoritative voice brings my feet to a halt.

"I need to go." My struggles against his vise grip are useless.

"Not so fast." He hauls me into the empty private dining room to my left. "What happened out there? Rourke seemed upset. Is everything okay?"

"No." The coldness in his eyes strikes fear into my heart. "Roman's a lead suspect in Lavender's murder. You wouldn't know anything about that, would you? I mean, you were the last person with her that night." My insides begin to quake. I've never been afraid of him before, but now, I don't like the cruel line of his mouth or his bruising grip on my flesh. "Have you spoken with the authorities yet?"

"I told you to forget about that. I don't know anything about Lavender's death. You didn't say anything, did you?" To emphasize the urgency of the matter, he shakes me hard enough to rattle my earrings.

"Let go." His fingertips bite into my bicep. "No. I didn't say anything."

"Are you lying?" The cruel face in front of me is unrecognizable. This man isn't my father. This man is a stranger.

"Why are you acting like this? Stop. You're hurting me." My voice is shaky but convincing. The pinch of his fingers eases from my arm.

"If you know anything, anything at all, I need you to tell me, Everly. It's important." His face looms above mine.

"The police searched their penthouse for evidence. They're going to indict Roman."

"Is that right?" He rubs the back of his neck.

"What do you know, Daddy? I can't help if I don't know the whole story."

His gaze searches my face. I rearrange my expression into one of sympathy. Inside, I'm quaking. His response could alter the trajectory of a dozen lives. "Lavender became a liability. She knew too much and threatened to talk. No one jeopardizes my position. No one. Not her. Not you. Do you understand what I'm saying?"

"Yes." His threat reverberates through my body and into my toes. My heart races. I've got to get out of here. I have to tell Rourke.

"Because I'd hate for you to get involved in something you know nothing about."

"No. I won't." I shake my head, easing away from him, creeping back toward the door. A waiter glances into the room, drawn by our raised voices. Father steps away from me and runs a hand through his hair. I seize the opportunity to escape, jogging down the hall toward the exit as fast as my high heels will allow.

On the sidewalk in front of the restaurant, I dig out my phone and call Rourke. An electronic voice answers. "I'm sorry. The number you are calling is no longer in service. Please check the number and try again." After a groan, I toss my phone into my purse.

Traffic clogs the street. Not a taxi in sight. At this rate, I'll be here forever. I dig out my phone again. Tears of frustration blur the screen. I draw in a steadying breath. My love for my best friend overrides loyalty to my father. I need to tell Rourke about Father's affair. He's going to be so angry with me, but Rourke deserves to know the truth. If Roman is found guilty, I'll never be able to live with myself. I try her office, her home, and her cell. No luck. As a last resort, I type out an email to her personal address. *Call me. ASAP. Important.* Until she contacts me, all I can do is wait.

When I glance up from my phone, Prince Henry is striding through the revolving door. He's coming straight at me. In the open air, his hair is blonder, his eyes brighter. My heart does a double flip at the way his gaze locks onto mine and stays there.

HENRY

OUTSIDE THE RESTAURANT, the sunshine is bright and hot, shimmering over the sidewalk. The street sounds assault my ears—a jackhammer from nearby road construction, honking car horns, a siren, various shouts, and whistles. The cacophony recedes at the sight of Everly. She hovers on the sidewalk, rummaging through her purse with the frustrated, jerky movements of a woman in distress.

I touch her elbow. "Excuse me. Is everything okay?" My security team closes around us, shielding us from curious onlookers.

"I'm fine." After more rummaging, she finds a tissue and swipes at her nose. Her red-rimmed eyes find mine. Electricity jolts through my body at the collision of our gazes.

"No. You're not." I touch her elbow again, this time letting my fingers wrap gently around her warm skin, ignoring the buzz of attraction skating up my arm. "I can see you're upset. I'll take you home."

"No. It's not necessary." She waves at an approaching taxi. "I'm not upset. I'm angry. I always cry when I'm mad."

I motion for him to move on. "I insist." My car pulls up in front of us. The driver opens the door. I nudge her toward the passenger door. "See? It's right here. Let me drop you somewhere. It'll make my day."

"Well, okay." She dabs at the tears caught in her thick,

dark eyelashes. "This is the second time you've come to my rescue." Her gaze hovers on my mouth, and I like it there. I like having her attention focused on me.

"It's my pleasure, Everly." Lust and the need for revenge war inside me. How angry would Don McElroy be if I turned his little princess into my whore? It's the perfect answer to my predicament. I can satisfy my sexual urges and piss him off at the same time.

The seductive scent of her perfume fills the car once the door closes behind us. Her fingers fly over the keyboard of her phone. After a few minutes, she sighs and throws her phone into her purse then tugs the hem of her dress down to her knees. The movement draws my eyes to her shapely calves. I can't help wondering what kind of knickers she's wearing beneath that dress. A thong? Lace? Satin? If there's a god, she's not wearing any at all. Then I feel guilty for lusting after her while she's in obvious distress. I shift in the seat to hide the growing tightness of my trousers and try to steady my thoughts.

"Where can we drop you?" I ask, wishing I had the balls to take her to my hotel. Once she gives the address to my driver, I raise the partition to provide us with privacy. The ooze of her tears has halted. "Is there anything I can do to help?"

"No. Thank you. There's really nothing to be done." She glances at me, smiling through her sadness, and I respect her all the more for the effort. "I'm not usually this emotional, but lunch…it was a fiasco."

"We all have those kinds of days." I squeeze the hand resting on the white leather seat between us. "My conversation with your father didn't go very well, either." Attraction surges up my arm at the glide of her soft skin against mine. The bones of her fingers feel fragile and small beneath my large ones. The need to protect her consumes me. "Everything will work out."

"I'm not so sure." The edges of her white teeth bite into the plump flesh of her lower lip. I hold back a groan. What I wouldn't give to hear her beg for my cock again.

We're silent as the car sits in stalled traffic. I can't take my eyes off her. A blush creeps from her neck, up her throat, and settles in her cheeks. Having her next to me is an unexpected dream come true. Her feminine presence fills the car, making me feel large and clumsy. She slips her hand from beneath mine to push the hair away from her face.

"I know it was you last night." My heart skips a beat at her unexpected confession. She tilts her head, gazing down her nose at me, waiting for a response.

"So much for the NDA," I remark dryly. Inside, I'm pleased. With our identities out in the open, life is infinitely more interesting. "Do we need to talk about it?"

"I don't know. Do we?" The boldness of her stare jolts all the way to my cock.

"Not really. Unless you have questions?" I lean forward, caught up in the flecks of green and gray in her blue eyes.

"Does Nicky know?"

"No. And he won't hear of it. At least not from me." In the afternoon light, her complexion is almost translucent. Sheer perfection. I study her profile, searching for clues about her feelings toward him. "Do you still care for him?" The idea hurts more than I care to admit.

"No." Her chin juts. This display of spirit is the cutest thing I've ever seen. She shifts in the seat to face me. Her knee grazes mine. A thrill scurries up my leg and into my groin. Her eyes narrow. "How do you treat women, Prince Heinrich? A man in your position must have girls lined up at the door, begging for your attention. Do you fuck them then throw them away like he does?"

Her question catches me off guard. No one talks to me this way, not even my closest advisors. "You're a cheeky wench."

"I'm just over the bullshit." She rests her head on the back of the seat. There's a note of weariness in her voice, much too heavy for someone so young. The limo changes lanes abruptly as a car cuts us off. She braces a hand against the seat in front of her.

"I don't fuck just anyone. You're one of a select few."

"Am I supposed to be flattered?" She swallows, like I'm making her nervous.

"I'm sitting alone in a limousine with you, breaking every rule of Androvian protocol, telling you that you're special. So yes, I want you to be flattered."

She shifts in the seat. Her eyes rove over my face. "Do you mind if I ask you a question? I could use an impartial perspective."

"Sure. Ask away." This is my chance to gain her trust. I'm not sure why it matters, but it does. I lean forward, curious to hear her story.

"What if you knew a secret about someone important in your life—something devastating? Telling this secret will ruin a lot of lives. But if you don't tell, innocent people will be destroyed."

Her question catches me off guard. Is she talking about her father? I need to tread carefully. An unwelcome thought plants in my head. What if our encounter was engineered by Nicky and Don as some kind of elaborate scheme to sway my political alliances? More than one future king has been defeated via his lust for a beautiful woman.

I take a minute to consider the possibility before answering. The hue of her eyes intensifies to infinite pools of azure. My heart skips a beat. I clear my throat. "I need more information. Has this person done something illegal?"

"Yes." The word is breathy and soft.

"Do you think he—or she—will do it again if given a chance?"

"Yes."

"The answer is simple. Innocent people must always be protected from those of corrupt natures." As a member of the royal family, I'm sworn to look after my subjects and shelter them from harm. "If you don't come forward, you're complicit in the crime by your silence. Those who stand by and do nothing are just as guilty as those who commit the offense, in my opinion."

"I was afraid you'd say that." A rueful smile twitches the corner of her mouth, taking my eyes there, making me yearn to kiss her. Except I don't do kisses. Not for her. Not for any woman. Especially not now, with the threat of Don McElroy looming overhead. She shrinks into the seat and crosses her legs away from me. Sunlight catches fire to the red strands in her dark hair. The pressure behind the fly of my trousers continues to grow with each blink of her lacy eyelashes. Memories of last night's clutching fingers and the scrape of nails down my back intensify the ache in my testicles.

I change the subject, hoping to distract myself. "Have you known Mrs. Menshikov for very long?"

"As long as I can remember." Her features soften, and a small smile tugs the corners of her mouth. "Grade school, middle school, high school, and college. She was my personal assistant for a while—until she met Roman."

"I've known Roman for years. Nicky even longer. If Roman married her, she must be someone special."

"She is." Her face falls. I've touched on a tender subject. Her attachment to her friend

During our conversation, the car reaches her apartment building and pulls up to the entrance. Too soon, my time with her draws to an end. She slides across the seat, eager to leave. I drum my fingertips on my knee. I can't let our first unmasked encounter end like this. Not now. Not when there is so much to be gained by claiming her.

"Would you like to come upstairs?" She pauses at the door to look back at me, surprising me again. "For sex, I mean."

"Pardon?" My stomach flips. I'm confident I misheard her.

"I said, would you like to come upstairs and have sex with me?" She peers through her lashes with those enormous summer sky eyes. "Look, we both know that's all either of us are interested in. And to be honest, I could use a distraction right now."

My throat goes dry. The afternoon has climbed out of the toilet and shot up to the stars. I can't believe my luck. I scrub a hand over my face. As she exits the car, the hem of her dress rises. A flash of toned thigh steals my common sense. She pauses on the sidewalk, throwing a glance over her shoulder. "Are you coming?"

$\mathscr{H}$ENRY

THE MINUTE I step over Everly's threshold, my erection tents my trousers. The thought of her tight pussy clouds my brain. Her backside sways enticingly as she kicks off her shoes and pads barefoot through the foyer. I ruffle a hand through my hair.

"Come on in." She tosses her purse onto a small table in the hall and motions for me to follow.

"You have a nice place." Her apartment is classy and formal, feminine but not frilly, with a good view of the park across the street. I trail along behind her. My palms sweat like I'm a teenage boy again. I search for something to say, anything to break the tension. "Have you lived here long?"

"No." When she pushes open the next door, we're in her bedroom.

My gaze locks onto the queen-sized bed, the cream-colored duvet and the rows of matching pillows. She turns to face me. In her bare feet, the top of her head comes to the bottom of my chin. It's too easy to imagine her on her knees, unzipping my fly and taking out my erection. The traitorous monster stands straight up, nudging my waistband.

"I don't normally do things like this." She waves a hand through the air. "You know, invite strange men up to my bedroom."

"We're not strangers, remember? I've already been inside you."

"I have a busy afternoon, so we need to be quick." Her lashes veil her eyes from me as she peeks over her shoulder. "Can you get my zipper?"

"Of course." After sweeping her hair aside, I pull the tab down to reveal a sliver of flawless porcelain skin. I trace a finger down the groove of her spine. Gooseflesh pebbles on the milky white surface.

"Thanks." When she faces me once more, the dress puddles at her feet.

I suck in an awed breath. She's wearing a nude bra, matching panties, and nothing else. My hands curl into fists to keep from touching her. A monumental effort, considering the ache in my balls. With each breath, her breasts rise and fall inside their prison of lace. I loosen the knot in my tie, remove my cufflinks, because—fuck me—this is an opportunity I can't miss. One more time. Just once and I'll be ready to move on. "Do you have a condom?"

"Yes." The way she rolls her lips together makes me think she's more nervous than she lets on.

"Great." My fingers rush over the buttons of my shirt, the belt buckle, the zipper of my pants. Her eyes follow my movements. I shed my jacket then toe off my shoes, knowing with each passing second, the lines between cunning and lust are blurring. It's not too late for me to make an excuse and leave, but I can't. Not without tasting her first.

"Let me do that." Before I can form words, her hands are on my belt, tugging the leather through the loops, shoving my slacks and boxers down over my hips. My cock, at full mast, springs forward, eager for freedom. Like me, he has only one mission in mind, one that doesn't involve leaving. She exhales. "You have a beautiful cock, Your Highness."

I can't help a moment of smugness. All men love compliments about their endowment. "He's eager to fuck that amazing pussy of yours." A smile tilts her lips. Her warm fingers wrap around my shaft and give a delicate pull. This is such a bad idea, yet it's perfect. We'll fuck. I'll lock her in as my mistress and be on my way in twenty minutes.

"Careful," I warn. "You're literally holding the future of Androvia in your hand."

"Being careful is overrated." Her grip tightens. I'm dizzy as she lifts on tiptoe, placing her lips next to my ear, tickling my skin with her words. Blood rushes out of my brain and into my cock until my heartbeat throbs against her palm.

An unsettling thought puts a halt to my desire. "Did your father put you up to this?"

"What?" Her eyes widen in genuine surprise. "Is that what you think? That I'm some kind of double agent?"

"Don't get me wrong. I'll fuck you either way, but you can't blame me for asking. Your appearance at the Devil's Playground, showing up at the restaurant today...those are huge coincidences."

"I met you at the Devil's Playground last night because you invited me. I accepted your invitation to prove to myself that someone other than Nicky might find me attractive. As for lunch today, it was meant to patch things up with Rourke, the one person who means more to me than anyone. I had no idea you or my father or Nicky would be there. If I had, I'd never have chosen that place." In a show of breathtaking defiance, she juts her chin. "As for Don McElroy—the only thing we share is DNA. Believe what you want, but that's the truth of it." As she speaks, her nails scrape lightly over my balls.

The last drop of blood drains from my brain and races to my dick. Everything about her beckons me like a siren, from the confidence of her voice to the steel in her backbone. Perhaps I've underestimated American women. I have no idea if she's speaking the truth, and I don't care. In this minute, I'd do anything, go anywhere, move heaven and earth to have more of her. A strange state of affairs for a man with power issues. I slide my hands over her shoulders and down her arms. She smells better than any woman has a right to. Her skin is velvety smooth and soft beneath my palms. I can give up control for the time being. Knowing she's affected by me is more than enough.

"How should we proceed?" I ask, satisfied enough with her answers to move on to more pleasant business. "Quick and dirty? Slow and seductive? Hard and fast?" I walk her backward toward the bed then ease her onto the mattress.

"You tell me." Her long legs part, letting me settle between them. The sensation of smooth thighs around my waist annihilates the last of my self-control. "I don't want to make any decisions."

"That's exactly the right answer." Victory intoxicates my brain. By the time I leave, it'll be with her scent on my clothes and the memory of her tight body beneath mine. I'm going to rule her pussy like I'll rule my kingdom, with relentless strength and precision. I fist a hand into the hair at her nape, making her look at me. Her blue eyes widen in surprise, but the flare of her nostrils escalates my desire. "Do you like that? Tell me."

"Yes," she murmurs. "I like a man who knows how to take control."

I smooth a hand over her waist, slide my hand inside her

panties. Dragging a finger between her folds, I find her wet with arousal. "You're soaked."

"I need this." Her hips buck up as my thumb slips inside her. "Tick-tock, Prince Heinrich."

"Patience, love." With my left hand, I trap both her wrists above her head. I want her squirming with need before I mount her. Her lips part to moan when I brush a knuckle over her clit. Just because our time is limited doesn't mean I can't be a thorough lover. Some people call me a selfish bastard, but I've never left a woman wanting. I press a kiss to her throat. "The lady always comes first."

"A prince *and* a gentleman." Her voice breaks as my fingers move faster between her legs. "You're a rare find, Your Royal Highness."

Power zings through my veins at the formal address. The title is respectful, subservient, and a little naughty. Everything I like. "Say that again."

"Your Royal Highness." The breathiness in her voice means I'm close to driving her over the edge.

"A man can be dominant and still be responsive to his partner's needs." Tiny moans punctuate her gasps, and nothing has ever been more seductive. My balls draw up from watching the edges of her teeth bite into her lower lip. "Isn't that right?"

"Yes. Oh, yes." The way her legs twitch suggests I've drawn this out long enough. I can't wait to hear her cries of pleasure when she comes.

"Too bad we don't have more time, beautiful. I'd love to put my mouth on this pussy of yours and make you beg for my dick." I release her wrists. Her hands go straight to my back. The sharp edges of her nails cut into my flesh, making me hiss from the sting. "How bad do you want it?"

"I. Need. To. Come." She reaches between us for my erection. Her eyes squeeze shut. Lacy black lashes fan over her cheeks. "Please."

Under different circumstances, I'd draw out her pleas, make her scream for mercy, but not today. Not with my bodyguards waiting outside the apartment door. Instead, I shove two fingers deep inside her, searching for the secret place I know will drive her mad. She bucks and cries out, letting me know I've succeeded. Her walls clamp down on my hand. The rhythmic pulse of her pussy is almost as satisfying as the promise of my own waiting orgasm. "That's right. You have my permission to come, Everly. Open your eyes. Let go."

Her eyelids flutter open. A dozen emotions flash through her crystal-clear irises. Sadness, anger, impatience, need. How I'd love to explore those feelings, especially the glint of rebellion. My greatest accomplishment would be to tame that side of her.

I fumble for the condom and sheath myself before driving balls-deep inside her. She's relaxed and sated, still riding the waves of post-orgasmic bliss. My abrupt intrusion brings a cry of renewed desire from her pouty mouth. The wet heat of her pussy almost drives me to come. I withdraw to the tip before shoving back in. Lord have mercy, she's a schoolboy's wet dream with her vibrant hair spilling over the white pillowcase and her perfect tits bouncing. Three slamming thrusts later, I slap her thigh. "On your hands and knees, lovely. Ass in the air. I want to ride you from behind."

She rolls to all fours. I smooth a reverent hand over the roundness of her bottom and kneel between her legs. "Give it all to me. Hard." She blinks at me over her shoulder. My cock pulses at the sight. When I don't move fast enough, she rubs her ass against my groin. "You're killing me."

"Careful what you wish for." With a groan, I pick up a brutal rhythm. The sound of our smacking thighs fills the room. I grab her hips for leverage and pound her like a madman. The bedsprings creak. She braces a hand against the headboard. By this time, we're both grunting and cursing like a couple of porn stars.

"Don't stop." She bucks, meeting each of my thrusts with an equal shove of her own. "Your cock is amazing." The headboard bangs against the wall, and I'm close. So fucking close. "Yes. Fuck me harder."

Her dirty mouth sends me over the edge. I grind into her, going deeper and deeper until I can't think of anything but her cries as she comes on me. My chest threatens to explode from my racing heart. Release rushes through my veins, heady and sweet. We rock together, milking the pleasure until there's nothing left. She collapses onto her stomach. I roll to one side.

"Unbelievable," I mutter. My pants are bunched around my knees, the condom still on my dick. I remove it, tie it off, and shove it in my pants pocket. A guy can't be too careful these days—I'm not leaving my sperm behind for any woman.

"Now I know what it means to be royally fucked," she says and chuckles.

"Tell me. How does it feel?" I laugh too for the first time in weeks.

"Pretty damn good." She stretches lazily, making her breasts jiggle. The satisfaction on her face is its own reward.

Across the room, my phone rings from inside my jacket pocket. The sound is an unsubtle reminder that reality lurks outside these four apartment walls. "Pardon me." I hoist my trousers and grab the phone. "I'll just be a minute."

"Sure." She heads to the bathroom to clean up, not bothering to cover herself. I can't take my eyes off the sway of her ass or her long, long legs. Her auburn hair tumbles down her back, knotted from our fucking.

"What is it, Shasta? This had better be important." I take care of business and end the call as Everly returns. In a matter of minutes, she's gone from sexy temptress to classy beauty. "You look amazing." She's wearing a clingy wrap dress that accentuates her curves. My cock hardens in a show of his appreciation, ready for another round.

"Thank you."

"I have to go, but I want to continue this conversation later." While she watches, I shrug into my shirt, button up the front, and thread the cufflinks through the holes of my sleeves.

"No worries. I've got things to do." She grabs my jacket from the chair and tosses it at me. Her abrupt dismissal shocks more than it stings. No woman has ever ousted me from her bedroom. Another first. The surprise must show on my face, because she clears her throat. "I don't mean to be rude. It's just that we both know this isn't going anywhere."

"It doesn't have to be that way. I want to see more of you." My mind is made up. I step forward, pull her hand into mine. The contact ignites tiny explosions up my arm. "I'll call you later." I don't have time for relationships or dating, but I'll make time for her. "We'll have dinner. I'll take you somewhere nice. Anywhere you like. Or maybe a long weekend in Spain? I have a villa on the coast."

"No." She backs away, shaking that thick, red mane like a lioness, and pulls her hand from my grasp. "Like I said, I'm done with men."

No one denies me, but I respect her for trying. Her rejection makes her even more desirable. I might've been able to walk away before, but now—now, I've got to have her, if only to prove to myself that I can.

"Can I drop you somewhere then? I'm heading uptown." It's the only excuse I can think of to keep her in my company.

* * *

TWENTY MINUTES LATER, the driver parks outside the entrance of Roman's skyscraper. "I'll just be a minute," Everly says through the opened door. "I'm not even sure Rourke is here. Are you sure you want to wait?"

"Go on. We'll wait," I reply. I'm not letting her go quite yet.

I watch her walk toward the door. The breeze toys with the hem of her dress, plastering the material to her ass and thighs and whips her hair across her face. She pauses on the sidewalk to gaze up to the top floor before pushing through the entrance. I have no idea what she's doing here, and I'm curious.

I'm still staring after her when Shasta knocks on the opposite window. She slides into the car on the seat across from me. The bun has come loose from the nape of her neck, and a flush of exertion brightens her cheeks. "I had to take an Uber, the subway, and walk two blocks to meet you here. Tell me why again?" she asks, breathless.

"Because I asked," I reply, unbothered by her irritation. She's paid handsomely for the inconvenience.

"Right." With a sigh, she withdraws a folder from her briefcase then takes a second to repair her frazzled hair.

"Did you bring the contracts?"

"Yes. They're all here. Ready for your signature and Ms. McElroy's. She just needs to sign all three copies. Once we have her consent, we can work out the logistics of trans-Atlantic commutes, accommodations, and scheduling conflicts." She rests an envelope on the seat next to me. "Do you want to look them over?"

"No." We've been through this drill with other women a half dozen times. Before I can begin a serious sexual rela-

JEANA E MANN

tionship, she has to sign forms of consent and non-disclosure.

"Are you sure about this?"

"Of course."

"It's just—I'm sure she's a lovely girl, but don't you think her situation is kind of complicated?"

"I know what I'm doing, Shasta."

"You've already slept with her, haven't you, sir?" Shasta's face contorts into a frown. "You make it very difficult to do my job sometimes."

"Your job is assisting me, not the other way around." Bickering with her is one of my favorite pastimes. I try not to grin at her irritation, knowing it will pass within minutes.

"Do I need to remind you what happened with Marcella?" The intensity of her glare sears into me. Maybe I underestimated her feelings on this subject.

"No. I remember." The drain on my bank account still stings. Marcella had been an enthusiastic one-night stand. I'd been young and foolish back then and disregarded the advice of my lawyers to get the proper paperwork before engaging in sex. Within twenty-four hours of the encounter, photos of Marcella tied to my bed landed on my father's desk. Needless to say, the King of Androvia was less than pleased. It had taken a seven-figure payoff and a host of threats to silence her. "I'm not twenty years old anymore. I've learned my lesson."

"Have you, sir?"

"Yes." The snap in my voice carries a hint of anger. "Everly isn't Marcella. She would never go to the press. I've only known her a few days, but I trust her. There's so much more to her than you know." Shasta opens her mouth to speak. I silence her with an upraised hand. "End of discussion, Shasta."

"Don't forget your conference call is in thirty minutes, sir.

I'll see you back at the hotel." Without another word, she exits the car.

I drag a hand over my eyes. Am I making a mistake? Maybe Shasta is right. I don't know much about Everly, her background, or her character. What I do know is that she's the best damn shag I've had in years—possibly ever. And it's not like we're getting married. This is a temporary arrangement.

"She's coming, sir." The driver speaks to me through the intercom. I straighten my tie and place the folder on my lap. He jumps out of the car to open the door for her. I can tell by the pinch of her mouth that things didn't go well.

"Is everything okay?" I want to gather her in my arms, but the warning in her expression gives me pause.

"No. Everything is *not* okay." With a huff, she settles back in the seat. Large black sunglasses hide her eyes, making it difficult to read her thoughts.

"Do you want to talk about it?"

The car eases away from the curb and into traffic. The length of a city block passes before she answers. "Roman has been arrested. Did you know that?"

"No. I wasn't aware." On an average day, Shasta scans the headlines and briefs me on pertinent news. I rarely watch television. "What's the charge?" My heart races. If word of our alliance reaches the public, the fate of our two countries hangs in the balance.

"Murder." She says the word with nonchalance, like she's talking about baseball or the lunch menu. Her voice is calm. The Manhattan cityscape flashes past the car window. She stares at the tall buildings, the busy sidewalks, and crowded pedestrians. "My father had an affair with Lavender Cunningham. I saw him with her the night she died. He should be the suspect, not Roman."

"Take off your sunglasses." I slide across the seat until my leg touches hers. When she doesn't react, I ease the frames down her nose and tuck them into my breast pocket. "That's better." She lifts her gaze to mine, slowly, like she's afraid I'll see her thoughts. I run a finger along the side of her face. "Is this the thing you spoke of yesterday?"

"You can't tell a soul. Promise me." Desperation rings in her words.

"I promise." I pull one of her hands into mine and run a thumb over the ridge of her knuckles. She's offering me a wealth of information on a silver platter. Only a fool would turn it away. "Whatever we talk about stays inside this car. You have my word."

"I saw Father with Lavender on the night she died. We fought about it. I threatened to tell Mom. He said he'd end it. The next day she was dead." Deep furrows form across her brow. "I have to go to the police, don't I?"

It takes a few seconds for the meaning of her confession to sink in. Don McElroy framed Roman for the murder to get him under control. I exhale and let my head fall back against the seat. Things have gotten much too complicated, but matters might be turning in my favor. A murder investigation and subsequent indictment would keep Don busy— too busy to interfere in Androvian business. "That's your decision to make, but if you do, you have to be prepared for the consequences."

"No one will believe it." Her voice is soft and remorseful. "But I can't let Rourke and Roman suffer for something my father did."

"Let's walk through what will happen." I find her other hand and pull both of them onto the tops of my thighs. The concern in her eyes makes my heart squeeze. A woman with less compassion—a woman like Kitty—wouldn't care about her best friend's welfare or the repercussions to the nation. But Everly isn't any woman. "You call the police and tell them the whole story. If they believe you and the evidence supports your theory, they'll set Roman free and pick up your father. If they don't, Roman goes to prison, and your father walks away. Either way, he's going to be very angry with you."

"I know. I've thought about this from every angle, but I don't see another option."

Watching the pain on her face starts a war inside me. I have Roman's alibi. My statement, combined with Everly's knowledge, would be enough to free Roman and put Don McElroy in the hot seat. If I come forward, Androvia will suffer, and I'm not quite sure any woman is worth the welfare of my subjects.

"This is me." She tugs her hands free, gathers her purse, and slides toward the door as the car comes to a stop in front of her office. The worry in her blue eyes slices through my chest.

"Nothing is going to happen right away. Take tonight and think about it." I tilt her face up to mine, wishing I could break my rule and kiss her.

"I will." Our gazes meet. A small smile curves her lips, one that doesn't reach her eyes. She cups my cheek in her hand. The softness of her palm resurrects the sleeping giant inside my trousers. "Thank you for everything, Your Highness."

The driver opens the door. The sounds of the city flood into the car; honking horns, the hum of traffic, occasional shouts. I let her go, the contracts still in my lap. The door thuds closed behind her. I make the driver wait until she's safely in the building before we leave. Once the car is in motion, I rip the folder in half and toss it aside. Shasta was right. This relationship isn't going to work out for either of us.

13

HENRY

THE PHONE RINGS a few minutes before the butler comes in to wake me for the day. I clutch my dick in my hand, my head swimming with fantasies of Everly. It's been over thirty-six hours since the last time I saw her and less than a minute since I last thought about her. Darkness blankets the hotel suite. The caller ID flashes with a name that chills my insides. Rupert, Chief Minister of the Inner Cabinet, would only call me at this hour for one reason. Before I answer, I draw in a last, steadying breath. Once I respond, my world changes forever.

"What's going on?" As I speak, I swing my legs to the floor. The soft fibers of the Turkish rug tickle the bottoms of my feet. I dig my toes into the plushness and wait for my uncle's reply.

"It's your father. I'm sorry, Henry. He's dead."

Shock knocks the grogginess from my brain. "Pardon?" Is

this some kind of nightmare? I wait for the pain to sink in, but it never arrives. It's hard to grieve over a father known for his cruelty and greed. Instead, I feel guilty for not caring enough and shame for my lack of devastation. I'm a horrible son. "How? Do you know what happened?"

"A sniper picked him off the deck of his yacht. His mistress is fine but shaken. She's being questioned now. You need to come home right away."

Memories of my father play on a loop through my head. When I was a child, I craved his approval. He had seemed larger than life back then, a boisterous but handsome man with limitless power at his disposal. As an adult, I loathed his narcissism. Despite our differences, I never wished an untimely death for him. I'm filled with sorrow for the loss of his life and the knowledge that we'll never have the opportunity to reconcile.

"Henry? Are you there?"

"Yes. Of course." I jump to my feet, searching for my trousers and a shirt. "Did they catch the shooter?"

"No. Whoever did it was a professional. No witnesses. No leads. We're working with Greek officials, but they aren't cooperative."

"How's Mother?" Not surprisingly, she couldn't be bothered to deliver the news herself. We've never spoken on the phone before—not when my youngest sister died of leukemia, not when I graduated from university, not ever.

"She's as well as can be expected under the circumstances." He pauses. Delicate innuendo thickens the silence, allowing me to read between the lines. In other words, she's wallowing in the bottom of a wine glass. "You need to get here as soon as possible. We need to make funeral arrangements, notify dignitaries and the royal court. Plans need to be made for your coronation."

The royal countdown clock begins to tick, marking the

last precious seconds of my freedom. I'm not prepared. I thought I had years, not days. McElroy's conversation echoes through my head. That bastard. In my heart, I know he's responsible for Father's death. I shove a hand through my hair, trying to steady my nerves. "I need to tie up loose ends here, then I'll be on my way. A day or two at the max."

"Time is of the essence. Until you're home, the throne is vulnerable. Whoever did this has a political agenda. I warned your father to be careful, but he refused to listen." He inhales a delicate breath. "Shall I contact Lady Clayton for you?"

"No. Not yet." The steel vise of my birthright tightens its hold on me. No more late-night parties. No more Devil's Playground. No more Everly. Her loss bothers me more than anything. Just when our relationship was becoming interesting. Regrets are pointless. This is my destiny. I've trained my entire life for this honor. Seven generations of Von Stratton men have sat upon the Androvian throne. Now, it's my turn.

"Don't wait too long, Henry." Rupert's voice lacks sympathy. No one likes Lady Clayton. No one but my mother, Don McElroy, and him. Unfortunately for me, she ticks all the boxes for a king's consort: pedigreed, connected, Catholic, and wealthy.

"I won't." Numbness blankets my emotions. Our engagement might have ended, but the business deal between us didn't. She's still the only candidate approved by the court for royal consort.

"We'll wait to hear back from you then." Rupert ends the call, taking my hopes for the future along with him.

Resignation mingles with dread and forms a knot in the pit of my gut. I scroll through the address book on my phone for Kitty's number. My thumb hovers over the call button. The cheating bitch will be ecstatic to hear from me. Even though I know I have to do it, I can't quite make myself follow through.

* * *

ONCE DAYLIGHT ARRIVES, my team scurries around the hotel suite, packing and planning, canceling personal appearances and social engagements. They're invisible to me. Most of them have worked with me for a decade. When I claim the throne, there will be even more of them.

"Are you okay, Your Highness?" One of the aids pauses from folding my underwear to check on me.

"Yes. Carry on." But I'm not okay. I'm bloody terrible. My grief has transformed into anger. My hands shake with the force of it. Don McElroy will pay for this brutal crime if it's the last thing I ever do. I'll use every resource at my disposal to seek my revenge.

"Your tea, sir." A woman in hotel livery places a silver tray on the coffee table. I wave her away. The tea in America is hideous. I haven't gotten a good cup since I arrived. It's one of the few things I dislike about the United States—that and the lack of real football, or soccer as they call it here. She whisks the tray out of my sight.

At the moment, I don't have time to chase down a killer. I have to find a wife. ASAP. As King Gustav's only son, my wife must bring political and financial gain to court. When Kitty took Nicky into her bed, I abandoned the notion of marrying for love. My mind drifts to Everly—my beautiful, redheaded obsession. Marriage to her would be heaven compared to Kitty.

"Can I get you something else, sir?" Another person waits patiently in front of me. "Fruit? Toast? Coffee?"

"Nothing." On this, my final day of freedom, I'd like nothing better than to barricade myself in this hotel with a bottle of scotch and Everly, but I have business deals to close, arrangements to make, and a funeral to attend. I wave him aside then change my mind. "Wait. Can someone get me an aspirin?"

My head throbs while my thumb hovers over the call button on the phone for the tenth time today. The man bustles away to grant my request. I rub my temples. I'd have someone else place the call to free up my precious time; however, something inside me balks at proposing marriage through a team of litigators. As I wait, I can't help remembering the first time I proposed to her—the flowers, the candlelight, the music. That was before I understood who she was and that she didn't really love me. She loved the Crown Prince of Androvia: his yacht, the castle, and perks of royalty. Not me.

I toss the phone aside. The butler returns, offering two caplets and a glass of water on a tiny serving tray. I place the aspirin in my mouth and gulp down the water.

"Pardon me, sir. I've spoken with your pilot. The royal jet is on standby for whenever you're ready to leave." Shasta's voice comes from my elbow. I jump.

"Good lord, Shasta. Make a noise or something when you enter the room. I hate it when you sneak up on me like that." My frustration boils over, spilling onto her. "If it happens again, I'm going to put a bell on you."

"It's my ninja skills, Your Highness." Although her face remains impassive, amusement flickers in her eyes. "They're undeniable."

Despite the ache in my chest and a burning desire for revenge, the corners of my mouth tug upward. "Come and sit with me. Would you like some toast or tea?"

"No, thank you." Her eyes brim with sympathy. "Sir, may I speak frankly?" The soles of her flat shoes move noiselessly over the thick rug as she approaches.

"Go ahead." With two fingers, I rub the deep grooves between my eyebrows.

"Call Lady Clayton. The sooner, the better. Then you can move on with your plans." She smooths a hand over the bun at the nape of her neck. "Delaying the inevitable will only prolong the pain. Rip the bandage off, sir."

"Would you marry someone you don't like?" I study her face. The lines around her eyes are deeper than when we first met ten years ago. Otherwise, she looks the same. Medium height, thick glasses, sensible shoes.

"I'm not the Crown Prince of Androvia," she replies dryly. "If I were going to inherit a kingdom, I wouldn't hesitate." When I don't smile, she clears her throat. "But no, sir, I wouldn't. You, however, don't have that luxury."

Once I'm king, I'll abolish the antiquated laws regarding marriage and divorce. My children—the ones I'm destined to sire with Lady Clayton—will never have to deal with such foolishness. Except I can't fathom the idea of taking that snobbish bitch into my bed—for crown or for country. The thought sickens my stomach.

I drop my head into my hands and groan. "I can't do it, Shaz."

"You can, and you will." Her hand squeezes my shoulder, one of the few times she's ever touched me. "Think of the consequences if you don't."

"How can I forget?" I'm the only son amid a half dozen sisters. If I abdicate, the crown goes to my uncle Rupert, a bastard more ruthless than my father. Androvia would be lost to another tyrant. No matter how much I despise Lady Clayton, I can't sacrifice my subjects.

"You're a good man. I hate to see you throw your life away on Lady Clayton. That woman will only bring you grief. But I don't see a way out of this."

I place my hand over hers. "God knows we've been through a lot together. We'll get through this too." Emotion constricts the walls of my throat. She held my hand during my appendicitis, rescued me from drunkenness after the end of my engagement, and always supported my choices, no matter how controversial. "If there were someone else—anyone else—to consider, I would." Desperation weighs heavily on my shoulders. "I thought I had more time."

"I know it's a long shot, but—" She places the envelope containing the investigative report on Everly in front of me. Our eyes meet. "Perhaps you're not looking at all the options."

14

HENRY

*U*pon my entrance to the conference room, everyone stands. The place is quiet except for the shuffling of feet and the clearing of throats. I've known most of these people for years, some of them since childhood. They travel everywhere with me and are my most trusted advisors. The legs of my chair scrape across the polished tile floor as I find my seat at the head of the table. "Shasta, you start."

"I ran an extensive battery of checks on Ms. McElroy, like you requested." She frowns at her tablet, forehead puckering.

"Go on."

"She's absolutely clean. No arrests, no financial problems, no legal issues. She's philanthropic and has extensive media training. And her mother is a cousin to the Queen of England which makes her of royal blood." Shasta removes her glasses and rubs the space between her eyes. "On paper, she's perfect."

I can't believe that fuck Nicky let her slide through his fingers. His loss, however, is my gain. "Excellent." I turn to my second assistant. "Richard, did you find a same-day marriage state?"

"Um, yes, Your Highness. Connecticut. There's a reliable, discreet Justice of the Peace who can take you in tomorrow." The overhead lights glare off his balding head.

"Wonderful. Make the necessary arrangements." A dozen pairs of eyes stare at me in shock. I stare back at them. No one has the balls to question my announcement—no one but Shasta. Her gaze remains locked on my face.

"And what about Lady Clayton, sir?" The calmness in her voice contrasts with the panic in her eyes.

"What about her?" Lady Clayton's nonexistent feelings are at the bottom of my growing list of concerns.

"By now she's heard of your father's death. She'll be anticipating your call." Shasta's practicality wears on my need to set the wheels of progress in motion, but I know it comes from a place of genuine concern for my welfare. "We don't want to cause an international incident. At the very least, you owe her a heads up. And speaking of your mother, she isn't going to like this."

Mother's fits of temper are legendary among the palace staff. She'll blow her perfectly coiffed top when she hears the news, an added perk of eloping with Everly. Nothing amuses me more than making her lose control.

I dismiss Shasta's objections with a wave of my hand and focus on the next assistant. "Janet, take care of the wedding band. Make it understated, tasteful, and elegant. Ms. McElroy can choose something more suitable from the royal vaults when we return. Harriet, I want a full media blitz following the ceremony. Once the word is out to the public, it'll be more difficult for Mother to object."

Harriet bobs her head. "Certainly. I'll call in a few

paparazzi to leak wedding photos. And, if I may suggest, it would be best if this appears to be a longstanding secret romance. We can say that Ms. McElroy's affair with Nikolay was a ploy to hide your relationship from the press."

"I like it." Although Harriet's the newest addition to my entourage, she brings a decade of experience with a Hollywood movie studio to court. She's been a genius at hiding or leaking related events to the tabloids when beneficial.

"Sir, I believe we have a problem." Shasta frowns at her tablet, grabs the remote control on the conference table, and clicks on the flat-screen telly mounted to the wall at the end of the room.

"Now what?" The boundaries of my patience are being stretched to the limit. Now that I have a plan, I'm eager to get on with it.

A female reporter speaks from a Manhattan sidewalk crowded with onlookers. "In a shocking twist of events, former Vice President Don McElroy has been implicated in the murder of event organizer, Lavender Cunningham. These telling photos were taken hours before her death and corroborated by his daughter, socialite Everly McElroy." Grainy pictures show a smiling Don standing alongside the now-deceased woman, his big hand parked squarely on her ass.

I inch toward the edge of my chair to catch the rest of the news spot. The journalist runs through the McElroy family's background. A powerful man. Lust and betrayal. I pity Everly. This is a media goldmine. The bloodthirsty buzzards will milk this incident to the fullest. Best of all, she'll be desperate for a shoulder to lean on. A smile spreads across my face. I happen to have very broad shoulders.

"Are you sure it's wise to link your name with this scandal?" Shasta dabs at a bead of perspiration on her forehead with a tissue.

"Good gracious, you look like you're about to faint." The color has drained from her fair complexion. "Get her a glass of water, would you, Janet?" I relax into my chair. "I could care less. Androvia is a long way from Manhattan."

Harriet leaps into the conversation, a sly smile on her face. "It won't be an issue. Not the way I'll spin it. To the press, Prince Heinrich will be the knight in shining armor, swooping in to rescue a damsel in distress. And Ms. McElroy will be the sweet, honest woman deceived by her evil father. It's all a matter of perspective."

"Harriet, you're a genius." My praise brings a smile to her face, showing the faint crow's feet at the corners of her eyes. I stand, bringing the other occupants to their feet. "All right then, it's settled. Everly McElroy is now the number one contender for my consort. Shasta, have the car brought around."

"Yes, sir." She taps out a text on her phone while trotting at my side. "Have you thought about your proposal, sir? A woman like her might not find your offer tempting. She has a life and career here in Manhattan."

"She'll accept. I'll make her think she doesn't have any other choice." As we board the elevator for the lobby, the pieces of the puzzle begin to fall into place. I'm going to marry Everly whether she likes it or not. For the rest of Don McElroy's short life, he'll know that I'm fucking his little girl, using her body for my pleasure, and enjoying every minute of it.

15

EVERLY

*T*hrough the heavy velvet drapes of my apartment, I stare at the throng of reporters and television cameras on the tree-lined avenue. They're everywhere—on the sidewalks, across the street, spilling into the park. I should be panicked, but I'm not. The weight of resignation dulls the sheen of rain on the asphalt below. This is my punishment for being an honest person. I grip the parted curtains until my fingers ache. The crowd is thirsty for blood —*my* blood.

Shrill sirens split the air. The cluster of journalists parts long enough to let the arriving police cars pass. All the heavy-hitters are present: CNN, FOX, MSNBC. I spy familiar faces among them, some I've even considered friends. They stare back at me, waiting, circling like buzzards around a dying rabbit. Meanwhile, I'm locked inside my apartment, a victim of the shitstorm created by my father.

Thanks to me, Don McElroy will be remembered as the

Vice President indicted for murder. The stain of his sins will taint the the family name forever. The thought is a steel band around my ribs, growing tighter with each passing breath until spots swim in front of my eyes.

The intercom buzzes. The front desk security guard, booms into the speaker. "Ms. McElroy, your mother is here to see you."

My stomach twists. The thought of facing her is a knife blade in an open wound. She deserves an explanation; one my father has no intention of providing. I draw in a deep breath, steeling myself for the worst. "Thanks, Ken. Please send her up."

"No problem, Ms. McElroy." Annoyance textures his words. We both know it's a huge problem. The media has been storming the lobby for hours, blocking traffic and annoying the other residents.

I pace the length of the living room, lovingly decorated with French provincial furnishings and antiques gathered in my travels. Yesterday, this apartment was a welcome oasis from the bustle of the city. Today, the pale blue walls feel like a prison, growing closer with each passing second. The more I pace, the more anxious I become. When the doorbell rings, I'm a frazzled bundle of nerves.

"I came straight from the airport." She brushes past me in a cloud of subtle fragrance: lilies, lavender, and citrus. I trot behind her, the way I used to when I was a child and try to wrap my head around her anger—anger pointed at me. Except, my mother doesn't do anger. The only sign of her displeasure is the straight line of her mouth. "Your father is livid. I hope you have a good explanation for your behavior."

"Nice to see you too."

Her gaze scans the room, picking out the flaws—too many pillows on the sofa, not enough space between the coffee table and the armchairs, and a million other things that no longer seem relevant. "I'm sorry. Good morning." The cool brush of her lips on my cheek sends a shiver down my back. Her tone is pleasant but doesn't fool me. "Aren't you going to offer me something to drink?"

"What can I get you?" Years of etiquette training outweigh the awkwardness of the situation. "Wine or champagne? I also have sparkling water or tea."

"I'll have a glass of Chardonnay, if you have it. Otherwise nothing. Lord knows I need something to calm my nerves." The skirt of her silk dress rustles as she sinks onto the edge of the sofa.

An outsider would never know we were parent and child by the way we present ourselves. The realization saddens me. What would it be like to have a mother who laughs and teases? Who gives hugs and kisses and comfort? As quickly as the questions arrive, I shove them aside. Speculation on this subject is a waste of time. Apart from my father's recent descent into hell, I can't complain about my upbringing. How many people would give their right arm to grow up in the halls of the White House? I attended the best schools, hobnobbed with the most influential people in the country, and circled the globe more than once. The President of the United States taught me how to tie my shoes, for crying out loud.

"I'm surprised you were able to get through the crowd." While I speak, I find the bottle of wine in the bottom of the liquor cabinet, the brand I keep for her visits. She watches me wind the corkscrew. My hands shake at the prospect of her disapproval. Judy McElroy knows how to slay a person with one look, her words sharper than any sword. "You could have called instead."

"My security team brought me through the service entrance." Her shoulders rise and fall with a heavy breath. In a graceful motion, she slants her legs, assuming a demure pose on the edge of the sofa cushions, poised as always in the face of chaos. "Have you spoken to your father?"

"No." Words can't describe the devastation in my heart. "I have nothing to say to him."

"He's crushed, Everly, and so am I. How could you betray him—us—like that?" Her manicured fingers intertwine on her lap. "I wish you'd come to me with this before you went to the media."

"You always take his side." I start to pour a glass of wine for myself, reconsider, and go for a short glass of bourbon on the rocks. Mother frowns at my choice; ladies don't drink bourbon, especially not during the day. Inside, I shrug. I'm already going to hell. I might as well enjoy the ride. One sip of the amber liquid shores up my courage. "Did it ever occur to you that he's not the saint he portrays?"

Her deep sigh holds a world of secrets. "I've been with your father for thirty years. I know exactly who he is—better than you, I might add." The way she arranges the hem of her dress around her knees reminds me of my thirteenth birthday, the day my father was sworn into office. She wore a similar outfit, the same pale shade of green, one that complimented her slender figure. As Daddy placed his hand on the Bible and pledged his allegiance to the United States, she winked at me. The random memory is both comforting and disturbing. Ten-plus years of the political spotlight have hardened her, smoothed away the variations of her personality, and honed her into a stranger.

"If that's true, then you're an accessory to murder." My temper begins to simmer. I take another sip of bourbon, this one much bigger, and revel in the burn down my throat. The heat reminds me of who I am, sharpens my focus. "And don't you dare act like this is my fault. He's the reason for this—this circus." I wave a hand toward the street.

"Calm down, sweetheart. He explained everything to me,

and I believe him." Her words hit me like a slap. I recoil. If she believes him, it means she thinks I'm the liar. A faint smile twists her lips, and it's so cold it makes me shiver. "This is simply a terrible misunderstanding. I'm sure there's a reasonable explanation for whatever you think you saw. All this nonsense could've been avoided if you'd just consulted with me first."

"I didn't tell you because Daddy asked me to keep quiet." There's no surprise or hurt or unhappiness in the smooth lines of her face, adding to my confusion. Nothing makes sense anymore. When my husband cheated on me, I was devastated. "You knew he was having an affair, didn't you?"

The light in her eyes dims the tiniest bit. She holds my accusing stare. "The women come and go, while our marriage survives. Your father's a virile man. If he needs more than I can give him, I'm willing to look the other way. As long as his dalliances don't interfere with our political agenda, I have no reason to complain. And this girl, she was different. Important. She had ties to Roman. The value of her information outweighed my jealousy. Whatever your father might've done was necessary to further our cause."

The world tilts. I grip the arm of the chair to steady myself. My life and the people in it have been illusions. "Growing up, you preached honesty and integrity to me, and it's all been a lie."

"Where did you get such a fanciful imagination? You certainly didn't inherit it from me." She shakes her head. I want to understand where she's coming from, but I can't. A line has been drawn between us, one I'm not willing to cross. "When I married Don, we agreed to do anything necessary to get us into the White House. We're a team, Everly. His successes are my successes. His failures are my failures. I thought you were a part of our team too."

Her confession knocks the wind out of me. I sink into the

nearest chair before my knees give way. The narrow oval of her face, the relaxed slant of her eyebrows, the tilt of her head—nothing suggests the slightest bit of remorse. Rage builds inside me, stoking unfamiliar emotions toward the woman who gave me life. "Daddy threatened Rourke. Are you on board with that too?"

"I don't condone violence." Her elegant fingers tighten around the stem of the wine glass. "However, I trust your father to do what's best for his career. There are bound to be casualties along the way." A small smile plays on her lips. "And it's not like Rourke is family. She's a sweet girl, but she's not destined for greatness the way we are. Your father and I tolerated your friendship because you had so few friends, and Rourke was easily manipulated. She's been a delight, but now she's aligned herself with those Russian mobsters and refuses to stay loyal to us. The sooner you disconnect from her, the better."

The full meaning of her words settles over me. Acid churns in my stomach. I study her eyes, looking for a glimmer of salvation. "How can you say that?"

"People like us can't have emotional attachments to outsiders." The coldness in her gaze turns my despair into anxiety. "This situation is entirely her fault. Take my advice. Sever ties. Do it today." She rises, crosses the distance between us, and puts a hand on my shoulder. "Go grab your purse. The car is waiting downstairs. Our publicity team has prepared statements for us to read in front of the media. You'll say you had a problem with your medication and didn't know what you were doing. Your father's people are dealing with the photographs. We need to get on top of the situation right away."

"I'm not going anywhere." I shrink from her touch. Disappointment burrows deep in my soul. My mother—the person who should always have my back—sides with the enemy. "I won't condone what Father did. I won't be a part of it."

"You'll read the statement. Grovel, if necessary." Her icy and commanding tone widens the breach between us to an insurmountable distance. "I'm not asking, Everly."

In the past, I would've never disobeyed a direct order from either of my parents. But I'm no longer that girl. The future of my soul lies on the precipice between heaven and hell. "No."

"I won't leave without you."

We glare at each other. Behind the polished veil of civility, I see her composure slipping, and it gives me a tiny sliver of satisfaction. "Get out." Taking her elbow in my hand, I force her toward the foyer. "You aren't my mother. You're a monster." I open the door front door. My mouth drops open. There, standing in the hall about to ring the doorbell, is Prince Heinrich Von Stratton in all his blond gloriousness.

Deep-set eyes bounce from me to my mother and back again. My heart skips a beat then another. His gaze bores into me until I have to glance away. The sound of his deep voice has never been more welcome. "I was visiting a friend in the building and thought I'd stop by. Is this a bad time?"

16

EVERLY

*a*ny other time, I would've been intrigued by a surprise visit from the Crown Prince of Androvia. The muscles low in my belly clench at the memory of his hands on my body.

"Aren't you going to introduce me, Everly?" Mother puts on a pleasant smile, the one reserved for heads of state. I've seen it a million times, but today is the first time it feels false.

"Prince Henrich, this is my mother, Judy McElroy."

"Please forgive my daughter's rudeness, Prince Heinrich." The fragile links of a gold necklace gleam beneath the chandelier lights as she dips her head in a modified curtsey. "She's been under serious strain these past few days. I'm afraid she's not herself."

"There's nothing wrong with me." Her comment is designed to rattle my self-confidence. She and my father are masters at deflection. To keep my temper at bay, I shut down my emotions. Numbness settles over me, welcome and liberating, and I smile at the prince.

"Is this a bad time? I can come back later." His cultured British accent resonates into undiscovered places within me. He sounds so civilized, so controlled, and offers an anchor amid the chaos.

"Mother was just leaving." The breath hisses out of her as I give her a nudge into the corridor. "Please come in, Your Highness." Opening the door wider, I step into the foyer and invite him inside with a sweep of my arm. As long as he's here, I'm safe from my mother's bullying. She won't make a scene in front of royalty. Threats are for privacy and never for external ears, a lesson I learned before I could walk.

"Everly, we need to go." The straightness of her shoulders dares me to defy her. Her voice lowers to a venomous whisper. "If you don't do this, I won't be able to protect you."

Protect me? From whom? A frisson of fear ices my blood. From my father? Until now, I never considered the possibility of danger from the one person in the world who should be my protector. Despite my misgivings, I can't give in. If I do, I'll become an accomplice to Father's treachery. "My decision is made. I'm not leaving with you. Not today. Not ever."

"Don't be stupid. You have a chance to neutralize this situation. I'm not going anywhere until you come to your senses." Her tone is softer and carries a hint of desperation. She gives Henry a sideways glance, followed by a polite smile. "We're having a bit of a family crisis."

"I understand." The sunlight streaming through the window catches the chestnut and auburn strands in his golden hair. Despite his admission, he doesn't leave my side. His presence is reassuring.

I lift my chin higher. "My senses are better than ever. You're the one with a malfunctioning moral compass." With each word, my boldness grows stronger. None of this is my fault. I'm the only person in my family who's done the right thing. Weariness tempers the rising tide of my rage. Unless I take a stand, my life will never change, and I can't go back to the way things were. "Mother, I'm asking you nicely. Please go, before I call security."

The three of us stare at each other. Prince Henry seems unbothered by the suffocating animosity in the air. I expect to see pity or annoyance in his gaze. Instead, I find compassion in the somber lines of his face. His footsteps tap softly on the marble floor as he enters the foyer. The chandelier reflects off the shiny surface of his black shoes. Once inside, he turns to face my mother, blocking the entrance, shielding me with his broad shoulders. "I believe you're no longer welcome here, Mrs. McElroy."

A shocked giggle clots in my throat. No one has ever spoken to my mother that way, especially not someone of his power and influence. I clear my throat, daring her to rebel.

After an uncomfortable pause, she nods. "Fine. Everly, you can consider yourself removed from our family."

"With pleasure." I slam the door in her face and lean my forehead against the cool wood. The enormity of what I've done hits me hard. Tremors wrack my body from crown to heel until my teeth chatter. My mother chose my murderous father over her only daughter. Never in my life have I felt so alone. Tears prickle behind my eyelids. I will not cry. I will not cry. I. Will. Not. Cry.

"Everly?" Prince Henry's deep voice reminds me of his presence. "Are you okay?" He must think I'm a complete train wreck. Then again, I just released a statement to the world admitting my hero father is an adulterous, homicidal maniac, and I had a verbal altercation with my mother in front of him. Why wouldn't he?

"No. I'm not." I'll never be okay again. Hiding the truth will only make me look dumber than I already feel.

"Come here." He turns my body to face him. Strong arms wrap around my shoulders. I close my eyes and let him hold me, desperate for comfort. The notch of his collarbone is exposed through the open collar of his dress shirt. My nose nestles there, a perfect fit. In my heels, I'm almost six feet tall, but he towers above me. The scent of clean linen and his aftershave remind me of quiet evenings in the Hamptons. His grasp is firm and soothing but not carnal. Still, a tingle of sexual awareness zings into my lower belly. Beneath the lapels of his navy suit jacket, his torso is solid. The warmth of his body seeps into mine. For the first time in months, I feel safe and protected.

Except I hardly know this man.

"I'm sorry." Gathering my composure, I push away and immediately miss the shelter of his embrace. "How embarrassing. You must think I'm a train wreck."

"Don't apologize." Judgment and pity are absent from his tone. I study him, intrigued. He's freshly shaved and smells of soap. Up close, auburn and chestnut strands run through his hair. "My great-grandfather killed his father to claim the throne. My uncle would kill me if he thought he could get away with it. I understand the dynamics of a powerful family." Of course, he does. Knowing this unfurls the strangling tension in my gut.

"I guess you understand then." His hair waves above his forehead. Desire flickers in a shadowy corner of my body. Another time, another place, I would've found him irresistible. The urge to run my fingers through those silky strands and tousle their perfection is beyond tempting. To curb the impulse, I clench my fingers at my sides.

"Unquenchable thirst for power can lead a man to desperate acts. Crossing him can't be good for your health."

Father's threats ring in my ears. My fear grows. What if I'm next? I don't want to believe my father is capable of harming my friends or me. Then again, I never thought he could commit treason against his country or arrange to kill his mistress. I swallow hard. "You've seen the news?" His head bobs. "Of course, you have. Do you think I'm in danger?" He doesn't answer for a long time. The ensuing silence increases my terror.

"Can we sit?" His gaze flicks from my face to the living room. I nod. Gentle fingers wrap around my elbow and lead me to the sofa where my mother sat moments earlier. Traces of her perfume linger in the air. The scent turns my stomach. He sits in the chair across from me, leans forward, resting his elbows on his thighs, and clasps his hands between his wide-spread knees.

"Are you asking for my help, Everly?"

"Maybe." The quiet concern in his voice stirs butterflies of anxiety in my chest. I'm so far out of my depth in this situation; I have no idea what to do, where to go, or whom I can trust.

"Do you have anyone you can call for help? A family member or a legal advisor?" I open my mouth, but he stops me with one sharp look. "Someone other than a Menshikov or one of your father's cronies?"

"No." The desperation of my situation clicks home. "I have friends—counsel—but they might be on my father's payroll." I underestimated the scope of his power once before. I won't make the same mistake twice. Everyone in my circle—everyone but Rourke—has ties to my father in one form or another. Even the prince. My fingers tighten on the edge of the sofa, making dents in the cushion. "I'm fucked, aren't I?"

"You're not truly fucked until the last shovelful of dirt hits the top of your coffin." He leans closer until his knees touch mine. Power thrums through his legs and into mine. "I'm going to ask you one more time, Everly. Do you need my help?"

Yes. The admission screams through my head, although I remain silent. I'm too proud, too ashamed, too stubborn to accept assistance from a stranger. For all I know, he's part of this craziness.

He seems to read my thoughts. "Right now, you're wondering who you can trust. On my word, you can count on me."

"I want to believe you." The nature of his relationship with Father has been unclear but obviously contentious. I place a hand on his thigh, in a gesture of trust. Electricity jolts along my arm. I snatch my hand away, curling my fingers into a fist. "Father always gets what he wants. Always."

Henry bends forward to hear the soft words fall from my lips. His gaze catches on my mouth and hovers there for the span of a heartbeat before flicking back to my eyes. I press my thighs together, afraid to acknowledge the excitement of having him so close. The lids of his eyes lower. "And what about you, Everly? What do you want? Tell me and I'll make it happen."

A familiar, unwelcome voice breaks the hold of Prince Henry's stare. "Well, don't the two of you look cozy." Nicky leans against the doorway, hands in the pockets of his skinny black pants. His gaze bounces between the prince and me before settling on my heat-filled face.

"How did you get in here?" I rise to my feet. This man has already crushed my self-esteem. The last thing I need is more of his bullshit. He's part of the past I want to forget.

He lifts a key in the air and jingles it. "I have this, remember?" In the flush of misguided obsession, I gave him a key to my apartment and security clearance. Stupid, stupid girl. A smirk curls the corners of his lips. "I just came by to return it, along with a warning."

Nicky is the cherry on top of an already miserable day. I cross the room and make an ineffectual grab for the keychain. He lifts it higher, dangling it a few inches out of my reach. If he knew how close I am to losing my shit, he wouldn't bait me. "Give it here."

He studies my face for a minute. His gray eyes give nothing away. I stare back at him, clinging to the last remaining shreds of my dignity. Ignoring me, he walks further into the room. "Good to see you, Your Highness." The angle of his nod holds grudging respect. "Everly, I'm heartbroken to see you've moved on so quickly. And Henry, you certainly didn't waste any time moving in on my girl. Then again, I suppose a man in your position doesn't have time to waste."

"I'm not your girl," I growl. "I'm not your anything."

"Don't let him get to you." Henry's words tickle the shell of my ear. I had no idea he was behind me. The hairs on the back of my neck lift in a pleasant shiver. When he straightens, his chest presses against my shoulder blades. "Return the keys to the young lady, Nick."

"Here you go." Nicky drops the keys into my palm and lifts his shoulders in an elegant shrug. His long fingers close around my hand. The metal key bites into my flesh. "And now for the warning."

17

EVERLY

Nicky's ominous tone turns my blood to ice. At my back, I feel the heat from Henry's body. We barely know each other, but I'm acutely aware of his presence in the room. My father once said that great men need no introduction, and now I understand what he meant. Henry owns the space, commands it, making it all too easy to picture him on the throne of a magnificent castle.

"Spit it out, Nicky." Henry's smooth growl echoes with the confidence of a man used to giving orders and having them followed.

Nicky walks to the window, taking his time, and nudges the curtain aside to peer down at the tree-lined avenue. In his true fashion, he draws out the moment for drama's sake, basking in the spotlight of our attention. "Word on the street is that your father bought you a ticket for the late show, young lady."

"Are you sure?" Henry strides to Nicky and places a hand on his shoulder, forcing him to turn his attention back to us.

"Well, I wasn't there, but my source is reliable." The playfulness has extinguished from Nicky's eyes. It might be the first time I've ever seen him sober. The realization escalates my fright to a new level.

"That's ridiculous." My ribs constrict, squeezing my lungs. Each breath sends shards of pain into my chest. I place a hand over my sternum to ease the tightness. "Would he really do that?"

"Maybe." Nicky runs a finger along the fireplace mantle as if he's checking for dust. "Believe me or don't. It's your choice. I'm just the messenger."

"Everly, look at me." Henry takes my hands in his, forcing me to face him. Worry clouds his blue-green gaze. "Your father is the head of a high-level group of men who control world politics through war and drugs. Whenever you see a third world uprising, your father is behind it. He snaps his fingers and hundreds—sometimes thousands—of innocent people die. He may have put a hit out on you."

"What am I supposed to do?" The last vestiges of composure abandon me. I glance around the room. I'm on the fourth floor with only one exit from the apartment. If someone slipped past security, I'd have no escape, no means of protection. "I don't have anywhere to go."

"My, my...look at the time." Nicky shakes his head and feigns a glance at his Rolex. "I've got an appointment on the other side of the city. You'll have to excuse me."

"You're leaving? Now?" I throw my hands in the air. This is so typically Nicky. He runs at the first sign of trouble. I have no idea what I ever saw in him.

"Afraid so." The corners of his mouth turn down in a melodramatic frown. He crosses the room at a swift pace. At the threshold to the foyer, he waves a hand. "Don't bother seeing me out. You two carry on with whatever you were doing when I got here. Unless you want me to join you. No?" He pauses to capture my gaze for a final time. "Oh, and I'd stay away from the windows, if I were you, young lady."

"What does that mean?" I ask, although I already know. The thought of a sniper's sight trained on my apartment causes my stomach to churn.

"It means you need to think very carefully about your actions from here on out. Where you go. Who you trust."

I've never felt so alone in my entire life. Always before, I've had friends and family around me. Aside from Rourke, I have no one. Even if I did, I wouldn't want to draw them into this dangerous circle.

Henry takes a seat on the sofa. The smooth fabric of his trousers stretches tight across his thighs as he leans back, spreading his knees wide, and rests an arm along the back. With his opposite hand, he pats the cushion at his side. "Everly, come. Sit. Pacing will only wear out the carpet."

"You should go." I press my palms together to hide the way they're shaking. "You're an important man. You don't want to get caught up in this. You could be in danger."

"I have security in the hall and downstairs. No one is going to get to you while I'm here."

The quiet calm of his voice soothes my frazzled nerves. I exhale loudly, letting the tension ease from my neck and shoulders. He's right. Now more than ever, I need to keep my wits about me. I give him a reassuring smile to cover my inner turmoil and perch on the sofa beside him. "Are you really here visiting a friend?"

"In my country, I could have you beheaded for questioning my honesty." Amusement dances in his gaze. Thick black lashes surround irises the color of the Aegean Sea on a stormy day. From childhood vacations in Crete, I know those waters are warm, beautiful, and dangerous, a fact I vow to remember. I can't let this man—any man—get under my skin. The men in may past are proof enough of that.

"Good thing we're in Manhattan then." A mouth like his begs to be kissed. Heat gathers between my thighs.

"Yes, lucky for you." The gap between us shrinks as he inches forward. He touches a strand of my hair, rubbing it between his thumb and index finger, before sweeping it over my shoulder. The slow, deliberation of his movements intensify the erotic aura surrounding him. "For you, I'm willing to show leniency."

Lord have mercy, this man is about to set my panties on fire. Two back-to-back failed relationships, however, have proven my poor judgment regarding men. I shut down the twinges of sexual attraction. From now on, my heart is on lockdown, no matter how hot or how sexy the man in question might be. I clear my throat. "Did you have a reason for stopping by, or is this a social call? You never said. If it's social, then I'm afraid I'm not very good company today."

His eyes haven't left me once since he sat on the couch. I want to look away, but I can't. Instead, I lean back. The incline of his torso ghosts my move, inching forward to keep the distance between us negligible. "I heard about your situation and thought I could be of assistance."

"I don't think anyone can help me." The sickening sensation of defeat returns to my stomach. Needing a reprieve from the magnetic pull of his body on mine, I return to the window. I hover next to the curtain, safely obscured from sight as Nicky's warning repeats through my head. Meanwhile, the police have erected barriers along the sidewalks to keep the crowd out of the street.

"I can get you out of here. Provide a place to stay until the threats from your father are dealt with." He stands beside me. The sleeve of his blazer brushes my arm, sending tingles to my fingertips. Together, we stare at the circus down below.

"I appreciate your generosity, but I'm pretty sure this mess is going to follow me to my grave." With sickening clarity, the extent of my punishment reveals an ugly future. My father is a bulldog when it comes to revenge. He'll never give up. I'll never be safe.

"What if I could guarantee your welfare? Would you accept my help?"

I study his strong profile. His blue-blooded pedigree shows in the sharp right angle of his jaw, his straight nose, and the height of his cheekbones. "You're serious? You would do that?"

"Absolutely." He turns to face me, clasping his hands behind his back. "I'm leaving for Androvia tomorrow. Come with me. Take refuge at the palace. The borders of my country are ironclad. No one will bother you there. Stay as long as you like. As my honored guest, of course."

A warning shiver runs down my back. His offer sounds too good to be true. Nothing in this world comes without a price, a price I might not want to pay. "You don't even know me."

"I know enough."

"I couldn't possibly leave. I have my family, my job, and Rourke..."

"Not anymore."

His words steal my breath. My mother is the head of the charitable foundation where I work, but I can't possibly continue under her direction. As for Rourke, she's found her happily-ever-after with Roman. I have no one to hold me here. The thought brings the sting of tears to my eyes. I blink them back, lifting my chin, unwilling to show my devastation to the proud man in front of me.

"There's no reason to stay here." Quiet confidence underscores his voice. He glides a fingertip along the side of my face, making me shiver, then captures my chin in his hand.

"Come to Androvia. Your every wish will be my command. I'll make sure of it."

A summer away might be the answer to my problems. The situation might change a lot in a few months. I've never been to Androvia, but I've heard it has high mountains, green pastures, and rustic thatched cottages. It could be fun. And the company of the crown prince would be a welcome distraction. Before I accept, it occurs to me that he never finished his previous train of thought. "You said two reasons brought you here. What was the second one?"

"I have a proposition for you."

Before I can respond, we're interrupted by the vibration of my phone on the coffee table. We glance at it. Fear and dread dance in my chest. "It's my father." Prince Heinrich picks up the phone, reads the screen, and hands it to me. "No." I shake my head, backing away like the phone might jump out of his grasp and attack me.

"Have you spoken with him at all since your press release?"

"No, and I don't intend to."

He palms the phone. A frown wrinkles his brow. "Maybe you should. Tidy up your loose ends before you leave with me. At least you'll know where his head is at."

"You're certainly confident of yourself, aren't you?"

"Arrogance is one of my best and worst traits." The phone falls silent for a few seconds before resuming its annoying buzz. I stare at it. One of his eyebrows lifts as he puts the phone to his ear and accepts the call. "Hello, Don. Prince Heinrich here. How are you?"

"No. Are you crazy?" I make an unsuccessful swipe for the phone.

The prince smiles, dimples dancing, and sidesteps my attempts to regain control. "What am I doing here? Visiting your lovely daughter." His eyes meet mine, brimming with mischief. "In fact, I'm glad you called. We were just talking about you." The prince holds the phone away from his ear. He lifts a finger, gesturing for me to be patient. "Are you threatening me, Don? Because I don't respond well to threats." He hands the phone to me. "He wants to talk to you."

"Everly, have you lost your ever-loving mind?" Dad's voice booms through the phone.

"My mind is better than ever, Daddy. Thank you for asking."

"What is that man doing in your house?"

"It's none of your business." Nausea builds in my stomach. He knows I'm at home, making me a sitting duck for anyone wishing me harm. In the back of my head, a countdown clock begins to tick. One of his minions might be on his way here, ready to cash in my ticket.

"Your mother says you've refused to make a statement. Tell me that's not true." The little girl inside me, the one who always sought her father's approval, wants to bend to his will. But I'm not a child anymore. I know the difference between right and wrong, and what he's done goes beyond evil.

"This is your mess, Dad. You clean it up."

The prince bends to whisper in my free ear. "Well done." His breath tickles my skin, sending pleasant shivers down my spine.

Father's tone softens, assuming the silkiness of a Svengali. "The crown prince is not your friend, my dear. You can't trust him."

"That's funny, coming from you."

He's silent for so long, I think he's forgotten me. My mind flits through memories of his kisses on my skinned knees, his strong hands holding me in the saddle of my first pony, the delight in his eyes at my college graduation. Did those moments mean nothing? I don't know how to separate the hero of my youth from the monster of my present.

"It's not too late. We can still minimize the damage of what you've done. Just come home, Everly. We'll face this situation as a family, the way we always have."

"If I don't, are you going to have me killed?" More than anything, I want to run into his arms, have him squeeze me tight, and tell me I've been a good girl. I wait for his denial. It never arrives. The truth hurts, stabbing me through the center of my heart, dealing a final deathblow to our relationship. I've never been a mean person, but right now, in the heat of the moment, I want to hurt this man the way he's hurt me. I run the tip of my tongue around my dry lips, gathering the courage. "Goodbye, Daddy."

I end the call and snip the last threads of connection to my father. The pain in my chest recedes, leaving a dull ache, like I've plucked an arrow from my heart and left behind an empty hole in its place. I give the prince a small smile, hiding the devastation in my heart.

He studies me in silence. No matter how hard I try, I can't deny the pull of his enigmatic gaze. After a few agonizing seconds, he rests a hip on the chair arm beside him and folds his arms over his broad chest. "You might be the bravest woman I've ever met."

"Or the dumbest." I head toward the attached dining room to gain much-needed breathing space. Henry keeps a respectful distance. The aura of power and sexual prowess surrounding him makes coherent thought difficult. He hovers near the credenza. The way his protective gaze follows me elicits warring emotions of desire and rebellion. Whatever his reasons for coming here, I can't deny that I like his attention.

This is my favorite room, a place for friends and family to gather on starry summer nights or chilly wintry evenings.

Bright sunlight spills through the glass to form colorful yellow puddles on the hardwood floor. I close my eyes and let the sun warm my face. For a heartbeat, I pretend everything is normal. When I open my eyes, reality returns. This is my life. Or what's left of it.

My heart stops at the sight of a red laser dot on the wall. Henry's gaze follows mine. Real fear drains the color from his face. He's at my side within seconds. His fingers encircle my bicep. With a firm tug, he pulls me to his side, into the shadows of the hallway.

"It's okay," he says, as much to himself as to me. The dot disappears. Maybe it was refracted light from one of the leaded glass windows or a reflection from a car on the street.

"I'll never be safe." Seeking comfort from the ugly truth, I wrap my arms around my waist. "He'll come for me, and there's nowhere I can go." Although this incident was a fluke, the next time could be real. Henry tightens his grip on my arm. He pulls me toward the hall.

"We're leaving. Now." With a hand on the small of my back, he nudges me into the bedroom. "Just grab the necessities. I'll send someone to pack the rest of your things." He talks on his phone in German while I toss an armload of dresses, toiletries, and a framed photo of Rourke into a suitcase. I'm too rattled to translate his conversation, but I pick up on words like urgent, danger, and security. Within minutes, we're being escorted to the parking garage by his bodyguards. He speaks to me in a soothing, confident tone as we're hustled into one of three waiting SUVs. "Do you have your phone? Give it to me."

Numbness blankets my thoughts and feelings. I place the phone in his hand. He gives it to one of his bodyguards. "Wait. What are you doing?" I reach for the phone, but it's too late. The man crushes it beneath his boot heel.

Henry takes my outstretched hand into his. "We'll get you another one."

The cavalcade races toward his hotel—or crawls, according to the whims of midday traffic. Streets and buses and storefronts blur into streaks of color. I can feel my old life slipping away with each passing city block. I scan the faces of the pedestrians, looking for a potential hitman who's eager to extinguish my lifeforce for a sum of money.

"You're trembling." Henry slips out of his suit jacket and drapes it around my shoulders. "Don't be frightened. You're safe. I give you my word."

Something tells me he doesn't give his word often, but when he does, he means it. My instincts tell me that I can count on him. What choice do I have? Even my personal assistant ditched me—via a text this morning—claiming she's too overwhelmed by the media storm to continue. I clutch the edges of the jacket, wishing I could curl into a ball and lick my wounds. The scent of his cologne clings to the linen. The lining still holds his body heat. "Thank you. I don't know why you're so nice."

"I could never turn my back on a damsel in distress, especially one as beautiful as you." His knee brushes mine when he leans back in his seat.

Gooseflesh ripples along my thigh. His tall frame over-powers the spacious interior of the vehicle. I give in to desire and lean into the crook of his arm. He holds me there and presses a light kiss to my temple.

Once we're safely inside his hotel suite, I'm overcome with nerves. My suitcase is taken to the smaller guest bedroom. Through the open door of Henry's master suite, the king-size bed beckons. A blush heats my cheeks. What price will I have to pay for my life? Another night with the Crown Prince of Androvia wouldn't be the worst thing to ever happen. In fact, the thought of his body on top of mine makes me tingle in all the right places.

"Everly?" The way Henry says my name suggests he's called me more than once.

"Yes?" I pray he can't read my thoughts.

"I'm going to meet with my staff. Will you be alright?" Concern warms his voice. "I can send someone in to sit with you."

"Yes. I'll be fine." I nod and smooth my hands over my skirt. His thoughtfulness stirs unwelcome desires.

"Make yourself at home. We'll dine in tonight." An air of command swirls around him as his broad back turns toward me.

"If you don't mind, I think I'll take a bath. A long soak sounds heavenly." Despite my frazzled nerves, I managed to notice the enormous jetted tub on my brief tour of the suite. Nothing heals the soul like the heat of a good bath.

"That's a great idea." At the door, he bows and disappears into the conference room adjoining the sitting area.

18

EVERLY

I fill the tub to the top with steaming water, fragrant lavender bath salts, and bubbles from the hotel spa, and slide beneath the surface up to my chin. My limbs float weightlessly. The sensation is delicious and seductive. I focus on my breathing, letting the tension ease from my neck and back. A nice bath has been a part of my evening ritual since I was a teenager, but lately, I've been too busy. Now I realize how much I've missed the quiet slosh of the water and the scent of herbs and essential oils.

When the bath cools, I pull the drain before adding more hot water. I do this several times, partly because it's heavenly and partly because I have no idea what to do with myself once I'm done. The question is answered for me when Henry knocks on the bathroom door. "Everly, are you okay?"

His deep voice startles me. I sit up, splashing foam over the side. "Yes. I'm fine."

"Are you decent? Can I come in?"

My nipples tighten into stiff nubs at the idea of being naked in front of His Royal Highness. "Um, I'm in the tub."

"I promise to behave." The door opens a few inches.

I slide beneath the surface, arranging the bubbles to hide my nudity. His gaze slides from my knees breaking the surface to the drops of water glistening on my shoulders. A pulse of desire hits me between the legs, sharp enough to make me sink the edges of my teeth into my lower lip.

When his eyes reach mine, they're dark and hooded. "You've been in here a long time. I was concerned."

"Have I?"

"Yes."

"Is your meeting finished?" The way his attention lingers on my mouth brings a second flutter between my legs.

"About fifteen minutes ago." The tip of his tongue drags along his lips. The gesture is seductive and primal, like he's dying for a taste of me. "I'd like to discuss a few things with you before dinner."

"Sure. Can you hand me that robe?"

"Of course." He takes the plush velour from its hook and places it in my outstretched hand. His gaze remains locked with mine, never dipping to the water. Although his tone is casual, tension outlines the sharp angle of his jaw. "I'll see you in the sitting room."

Stress creeps back into my muscles. What if something's wrong? What if he's changed his mind? I have no Plan B to fall back on. I take my time getting dressed, lingering over the damp strands of my hair, twisting them into a loose braid at the back of my neck. When I return to the sitting room, Henry is standing next to the fireplace, eyebrows drawn together. The sun has dropped in the sky, casting long shadows over the city. "I hope I didn't keep you waiting."

"It was worth it." His gaze slides over my breasts and hips. I chose a sapphire blue wrap dress that compliments my curves. Nothing is revealing about the V-neckline or the mid-length hemline, but the heat in his eyes cuts through the filmy fabric.

"Thank you." With each passing moment, I'm more and more convinced that he's going to expect sex in exchange for his protection, a price I'm willing to pay. He's virile, cocky, and oozing sexuality.

"Have a seat." He gestures to the chair in front of him.

"Do you mind if I have a drink while we talk?" The crystal decanter of liquor on the bar draws my attention. I've never been a serious drinker, but now might be the time to reconsider sobriety.

"Yes, I mind."

I draw back, startled by his direct refusal.

He takes my hand and leads me to the chair. "Sit. I need you sober and in complete possession of your faculties for this conversation."

Panic sucks the moisture from my mouth. Something's wrong. Maybe he's going to rescind his offer. Shit. I should've come up with a better plan than nothing. I muster a smile before balancing on the edge of the chair. "Sure."

He's changed from his suit into a black sweater. The clingy knit outlines the swells and dips of a taut abdomen and bulging pectoral muscles. I clear my throat and try not to stare. His movements are slow and deliberate as he relaxes into the cushions of his chair. "I have a proposition for you, Everly. It might sound a bit unorthodox, but it's a serious offer, and I'd like you to consider it as such."

"Alright. I'm listening." Defensive hackles lift on my neck. He's been a perfect gentleman all day. Then again, my judgment of men has always been weak. At this moment, I miss Rourke more than ever. She's always been a voice of reason for me.

"My father passed away this morning."

"I'm so sorry. Is there anything I can do?" Even as I speak the words, I realize how useless the gesture is. I'm in no position to help anyone. "I feel so selfish." I've been so consumed with my own problems that I failed to ask about his welfare. "Are you okay?" In a way, I've lost my father too.

"I'm fine. Thank you. I appreciate your offer, and yes, there is something you can do." He slides forward, resting his forearms on his thighs, leaning toward me. A shiver runs down my back, one filled with heat. My skin sizzles under the light caress of his fingertips over my knee. His intense gaze draws me in. My body angles toward him. "When I arrive in Androvia tomorrow, I'll be king, but only if I'm married."

My brain races to keep up. He's getting married. Once again, I've misread his signals. He's not attracted to me; he's kind. "You have a fiancée, and I'm in the way." How awkward. To my surprise, I'm more than a little disappointed. Of course, he's got someone. He's too yummy to be single. "It might be a little awkward, but I can stay out of your way."

"No, I'm not engaged." He strokes his chin, expression pensive. "And I need to be. I thought I'd have time to find someone suitable. Now, I'm down to the wire. There are a few candidates, but I find most of them untenable at best."

"You mean, love isn't an option for you." A life free of romantic entanglements sounds liberating. The full impact of his words hits me. "Wait. You're not suggesting what I think you're suggesting. Are you?"

"Listen to me, Everly." He takes my hands in his. "You're smart, philanthropic, and well-educated. You speak five languages—"

"Six," I interject.

"You understand diplomatic protocol, and you're not intimidated by powerful people. The events of the past twenty-four hours have proven that."

I can't stop staring at his thumb as it strokes the back of my hand. The roughness of his palms contradicts with the shine of his well-manicured nails. I can't help flashes of how his hands felt on the insides of my thighs or cupping my breasts. His touch distracts me from the agenda behind his words. "You know a lot about me."

"Enough." The fabric of his slacks whispers over the velvet sofa cushions as he slides closer. His knees bracket mine. "Marry me, Everly." His thumb swirls around my knuckle, over the blue vein, down to my wrist. Back. Down. Over. Each stroke elicits a new round of tingles between my legs. The moment it stops, his words hit home.

"Are you crazy?" I press a hand on my sternum to calm the erratic rhythm of my heart.

"My staff certainly thinks so." He squeezes my hands enough to focus my attention.

"We don't know each other. We aren't in love."

"That's what makes the situation ideal. This is a business arrangement. I need someone who can handle herself without the mess of emotions. You're more than qualified. In fact, you're perfect." His words buzz inside my head, eddying with the powerful buzz of desire. "I know this is unconventional but think about it. You have nothing holding you here. You can come to Androvia and start over as my queen. You'll have the protection of an entire nation. I'm offering you wealth and power beyond your wildest dreams. As my consort, you'll be able to champion the charities of your choice. You can change laws. You can make a difference." The low, hypnotic cadence of his voice seduces me in ways I've never imagined possible. "*We* can make a difference."

"I—I don't know what to say." *Say yes.* The sinful reply hovers on my lips.

"If things were different, I'd wine and dine you, shower you with gifts, court you properly, but time has run out." The earnestness in his eyes plummets to the pit of my stomach. "Be my wife." My head swims with the intoxicating proposal. "No one will ever disrespect you again. You can flip a big, fat middle finger at your father. Think about it, Everly. All you have to do is say yes."

19

EVERLY

My mind races with a thousand reasons to refuse his offer, but another part of me—the reckless, heartbroken, angry part—rushes to accept. This is a once-in-a-lifetime opportunity. Like I've hit the husband lottery. With his status as a platform, I could start a new philanthropic organization to help the disadvantaged. Charity has always been a massive part of my life. At the age of fifteen, I started a foundation for homeless horses and progressed to helping the victims of sex trafficking by the age of nineteen. Although my mother claims the Wings of Freedom Foundation as her own, the idea was mine. Years of hard work have made the charity successful. I hate to toss my efforts aside, but there's no way in hell I'll partner with her again, even for such a worthy cause.

"The wheels of your brain are turning. I see it in your eyes." One corner of his mouth curls in a smirk. "What are your dreams, Everly? Tell me, and I'll make them a reality."

The color of his irises morphs from dancing blue-green to soft azure.

I stare into their depths, desperate to read his thoughts. If he's sincere, I'd be a fool to turn away his help. "I want to help the less fortunate. I want to provide resources for the poverty-stricken. Give aid to those in need. Offer hope to the disadvantaged."

The warmth of his hands heats my palms, travels up my forearms, and settles in my chest. He inches closer. The scent of his cologne wafts between us, subtle yet uniquely him. "You can create a new foundation to replace the one with your mother." The smooth fabric of his slacks tickles against my bare knees. "I'll make a start-up contribution. Say, five hundred thousand?"

I've been around business people long enough to know we've passed the offer stage and progressed into bargaining. My mind races through overhead, staffing, and campaign costs. "I'll need two million."

"One-point-five." His answer comes back immediately, like he was prepared for my counteroffer.

"I want a salary." If things go wrong, the extra money will help set up a new life. My hands shake with increasing ferocity until he draws them to his thighs. The muscles beneath my palms are hard and sculpted. "Not money from the foundation. From you."

"You'll have access to an account with unlimited funds for your personal needs. Androvia might be small, but it's one of the wealthiest countries in Europe. Of course, our children will have a sizable trust, and the firstborn son will inherit the throne."

"Children?" The word is a faint echo in the large hotel suite. My heart does a ridiculous dance. I've always wanted a family. My ovaries swoon at the prospect of royal babies.

"Yes, Everly. We'll need to have sex. It's a requirement."

His gaze dips to my mouth before flitting back to my eyes. "One I'll enjoy very much."

Lord have mercy. An unexpected flutter hits me between the legs. I dig the edges of my teeth into the left side of my cheek to stop a gasp. The prospect of having his large body on top of mine, dominating me, schooling me on sex, sends heat rushing to the tips of my toes. It takes every ounce of my waning self-control to focus on something other than the sensual way he licks his lips.

His thumb resumes its leisurely exploration of my hand. "You already understand my need for control in the bedroom. I'll expect you to submit to me sexually whenever —wherever—I ask. That part is non-negotiable."

Oh, God. The pulsing of my pussy destroys the last bits of reasoning ability. "This power-play thing is new to me. What if I decide I don't enjoy it?" It's a stupid question. Everything about him, from the sensual curve of his mouth to the aura of sin in his eyes, reeks of sexual prowess. And if our previous encounters are any indication, he has much more to show me.

He edges forward, moving with predatory slowness, like he doesn't want to scare me. One of his hands slips to the back of my head. He wraps the length of my braid around his wrist then digs his fingers into my nape. A startled gasp pops from my lips. He's so close now. The heat of his breath puffs against my face. My ragged breathing breaks the silence in the room. I swallow, fighting to maintain control.

"Oh, you'll enjoy it." His lips press against the left corner of my mouth; soft and teasing. "I won't have it any other way." A second kiss lands on the opposite corner. Shivers of delight skitter along my spine. The tip of his tongue flits over the center of my lips. My nipples tighten until they sting. "I guarantee it."

"You're very sure of yourself." I close my eyes to savor the tug of his teeth on my earlobe, the tickle of his breath in my ear.

"Bedding you will be the best part of this arrangement—for both of us."

Unable to resist any longer, I turn my head, seeking his lips. Our mouths meet in a hot, wet kiss. I groan at the glide of his tongue over mine. His fingers tighten in my hair. He uses his grip as leverage to angle my head, deepening the kiss, taking more than I want to give. My hands find the tops of his thighs and clutch the smooth fabric of his trousers. I planned to hold a part of myself back from him, but his eager lips and tongue make it impossible. Too soon, he pulls away, leaving me panting. The color of his eyes deepens, hinting at dangerous darkness in their depths. It's our first and only kiss.

"You taste even sweeter than I imagined," he says, staring at my mouth. A blush heats my face. "I've thought about kissing you every day since I first saw you." The confession startles both of us. He releases my hair and shoves back in his chair. Cool air drifts between us. "Sexual chemistry won't be a problem for us."

My hands are still gripping his thighs. I unclench my fingers and drop them into my lap. While my heart continues to race, I struggle to regain a business-like air. I smooth hand over my hair. "And what is the downside to this situation? You make it sound like a true fairytale."

"Well—" His throaty chuckle gives him a boyish air. "You'll have to deal with my mother. She can be quite the handful. And you'll have to put up with me and my need for dominance. I've been told that I can be difficult and demanding." His lips are red from our kiss. The dimples bracketing his mouth dance.

"And if we hate each other?" One of his eyebrows lifts at the directness of my question. "A good kiss doesn't make a successful marriage. We'll need more than sexual attraction. Believe me, I know. I have a divorce decree and a handsome ex-husband to prove it."

"I'm offering you respect and affection without the entanglement of love. There won't be any messy emotions to impede our relationship. I can't give you more than that."

A note of sadness sparks in the depths of my soul. If we marry, I'll be giving up my fantasies of romance and love. Is this really what I want? A loveless union with a stranger? Sure, he's a future king, but is that enough?

The practical side of my mind rejoices. No more hurt feelings. No more misunderstandings. The idea of a drama-free partnership sounds idyllic. "And what if I change my mind?"

"Is there an escape clause, you mean?" A smile dances on his lips.

"Yes."

The amusement slips from his expression. "I ask for a one-year commitment. We can discuss dissolution after that time, if you desire."

One year isn't a long time. How bad could it be? I'll have my new foundation to keep me busy, and he's easy on the eyes, that's for sure. A year would give me plenty of time to deal with my father and the fallout from his murderous tendencies. "If things turn out badly, I'll need some sort of compensation to fall back on."

"Of course." He strokes his chin, keeping his gaze locked with mine. "Keep your apartment. You can have whatever possessions you acquire during our marriage. And I'll make sure you have a generous sum to pad your bank account."

"Can I get this in writing?"

"There you go—doubting my word again." The tension between us thickens the air, making it hard to breathe. He chuckles. "I'll have the documents drawn up."

My head whirls with the details of an arranged marriage. My demands might sound superficial to some people, but no matter what happens, I don't want to be left penniless. "This is all so sudden. I need time to think."

"You have tonight." He stands, towering over me. With his left hand, he tilts my chin up to look at him. The dominating maleness in his stance reminds me of the undeniable pull of attraction between us. "I'd give you more time, but we leave tomorrow. I need to be married when my feet hit Androvian soil."

The urgency in his words sets butterflies to twitter in my stomach. Whether I have an hour or a month, my answer will be the same. I'm going to accept, but I don't want him to know how desperate I feel. "Thank you. I appreciate it."

"It's my pleasure." The way his voice draws out the final word makes my nipples tighten. His thumb caresses my cheek as he withdraws his hand from my chin. "Regardless of your decision, you'll still have my protection from your father."

"I don't understand why you're so generous. It scares me a little."

"Don't mistake my actions for kindness. I'm not a nice person. I take what I want. You should know that about me. The sooner you realize what kind of man I am, the better for both of us."

His words haunt me long into the night. I lie awake, staring at the ceiling, weighing my options. If I pass up this opportunity, will I regret it? I've certainly come to regret many things in the past year: a failed marriage, humiliation by Nicky, devastation from my father. Marrying a prince seems trivial compared to those fiascos. The more I consider the prospect, the more confident I become. God has given me a chance to start over with a new home, new husband,

and new life. What kind of fool turns her back on an offer like this?

The clock on the nightstand says it's past two in the morning. Now that I've made my decision, my stomach growls. I've barely eaten in two days, and I'm starving. The hotel slippers cuddle my feet as I sneak down the hall toward the kitchen. If I'm lucky, the leftovers of our dinner are in the fridge. Henry's door is cracked, but the room is dark. His deep voice rumbles through the silence, too low to understand.

As I pass his door, he calls out to me. "Everly? Are you okay?"

I flinch. "Yes. I'm hungry."

"Come here." His voice is rusty, like he's been sleeping.

"Did I wake you?" Why, why, why didn't I stay in my room? Conversations with His Royal Highness have proven to be emotionally exhausting.

"Just do it, Everly."

After a heavy sigh, I push the door open. He's lying shirtless on the bed, propped up against a mountain of pillows, phone to his ear. Blue moonlight spills through the open window, highlighting the dips and swells of his bare, rippled abdomen. Drawstring pajamas hang low on his hips, low enough to show the definition of muscle below his hipbones and a dark trail of hair leading from his navel into his pants.

"I'll call you back." He ends his call and tosses the phone onto the bed. My gaze finally reaches his. The sight of his messy hair and hooded eyes creates chaos between my thighs. He's golden, glorious, and godly, the total package. "Can I have something brought up for you?"

"What?" No matter how hard I try, I can't stop staring at him.

"Food? I can call the kitchen." One corner of his mouth

twitches. The bastard knows how the sight of him is affecting me. "Or did you need something else?"

"No. I'm fine. I'll just grab some cheese and crackers." My toe snags on the threshold. I stumble backward. An awkward grab at the doorframe keeps me from tumbling into the hall.

"Suit yourself." The heat of his gaze slides down my body, through the open front of the robe, admiring my negligee. The silk clings to my braless breasts and panty-free hips. I freeze. Silence roars in my ears, broken by the erratic thudding of my heart. His smile broadens, wicked and taunting. "Did you have something else to say?"

"No. I mean, yes." I grip the doorframe until my fingers ache. "My answer—it's yes. I'll marry you."

* * *

This is the end of *The Royal Arrangement* and the beginning of Everly and Henry's story. Thank you for reading. Keep going to experience the first chapters of <u>The Rebel Queen.</u>

* * *

EVERLY

"I do." The wedding vow tumbles off my tongue, barely more than a whisper, sealing my role in a new and dangerous game, while my mind screams, I don't. A glance around the judge's chamber reveals a handful of strangers; various royal aides, assistants, and my bridegroom. I shift from one foot to the other, wanting to run, knowing I can't. The judge lifts an eyebrow. The lump in my throat threatens to choke me. No doubt, the honorable woman thinks I'm a gold-digging, traitorous slut, out to bag a wealthy husband. Nothing could be farther from the truth. I'm trapped in a terrible situation and chose the best option available: marriage to a gorgeous royal rogue, one who happens to be filthy rich.

"By the power vested in me by the state of Connecticut, I pronounce you husband and wife." The tension around the judge's mouth eases as she looks at Prince Heinrich Gustav Wilhelm Von Stratton. This fantastic specimen of virility will soon be the King of Androvia. Everything about him is sharp and hard from the cut of his expensive navy suit to the width of his broad shoulders. Short blond hair glitters beneath the courthouse lights. And his lips? Don't get me started. They're made for sin and stolen midnight kisses. The judge's tone softens, almost affectionate, as she completes the impromptu ceremony. "Prince Heinrich, you may kiss your bride."

His grip tightens on my hands. I'd run, but there's nowhere to go. No one who'll have me. No one but him. God knows why he chose to marry me when he could have any woman he wants. My breath catches. He leans forward and drops his gaze to my mouth. I expect a brief peck. What do I get? Two warm, soft lips part mine and a gentle tongue slips between my teeth. I don't want to like it, but I do. I lean into him, slide my hands up his firm chest, and curl my fingers into his lapels to bring him closer. My breasts flatten against the luxurious linen jacket. He tastes like cherries, smells like springtime, and feels like a man should, firm and unyielding. His palms drop to my waist, hovering in the small of my back, claiming me. Heat builds between my legs. The thoughts whirling behind my closed eyelids melt into sparkling colors. This is more than a kiss. It's a declaration of ownership. He owns me—in more ways than one—and he knows it.

"Ahem." From far away, someone clears their throat.

I don't want to let go. With my eyes shut and his arms around me, I can pretend that we're an average couple, that my life isn't a bucket of shit, and this isn't a huge mistake.

The prince ignores the interruption. He tightens his hold, deepens the kiss, and bends me backward. I hang onto his lapels to keep from losing my balance. A moan tickles my throat. Blood rushes into my breasts and thighs. My body knows him, wants him. I strain for more of his heat, eager to get nearer. He withdraws his mouth and steps back. Fresh air fills the gap between us. My nipples sting. Their tight points jut through the filmy white silk of my borrowed wedding dress. A camera flashes. I blink away the spots. Henry keeps his hands on my waist until I've regained my balance then retreats altogether, leaving me alone and bewildered in front of the judge.

"Are we done here?" A hint of Swedish inflection lurks beneath Henry's haughty British accent.

"Yes. Congratulations." The judge's voice floats outside the realm of my befuddled mind. Congratulations for what? For marrying a man I've encountered only a handful of times? For bagging the future King of a country the size of New Jersey? If she knew the desperation behind my decision, she'd retract her words.

"Let's go." Henry pivots on his heel and strides toward the exit.

In a daze, I follow His Royal Highness down the aisle and out the courthouse doors. My high heels click on the sidewalk. Everything seems too bright and surreal. I lift a hand to shield my eyes from the brilliant sun. Once the spots clear from my eyes, the dancing colors of daffodils spill over the edges of giant terra cotta pots near the street. Spring, my favorite season, has arrived in full force. I love the sight of budding trees and blooming flowers, and the hopefulness they bring for a lovely summer. But not now. Not today. Today, I feel like a part of me has died, a piece I'll never get back.

"Everly?" Christian, my only guest for the ceremony, grabs my hand.

"I'll have the dress sent back to you." The colors of the day whirl around me. It reminds me of riding a merry-go-round, spinning out of control, moving too fast for my equilibrium.

"Fuck the dress." He spits out the declaration in a deep and uncharacteristic growl. "You're pale as a ghost. Are you sure about this? It's not too late. Say the word, and we'll leave. Right now. No questions asked."

With only a few hours of notice, Christian had found a wedding dress and flew with us from Manhattan to Connecticut on Henry's helicopter. That's the kind of friend he is. Warm, caring, practical. Concern eddies in his eyes. His hands sandwich mine, squeezing until I exhale the breath I'd been holding.

"I'm okay." The words are as much for my sake as his. "Thank you for coming. You're the best." Tears sting behind my eyelids. Do not cry. I blink, gathering the last remaining shreds of internal fortitude.

"You know, I'm here for you, right? If you need anything —anything at all, call me. I'll be on the next plane to Androvia." His mouth straightens into a fierce line. We both know it's a lie. Not because he's dishonest, but because I'll be on the other side of the world in a war-torn country with a fearsome husband while he's in Manhattan.

I cling to his hand, the last remnant of my old life, feeling like a child about to leave for the first day of school, uncertain and tremulous. We've been friends forever. He's organized my wardrobe, given me advice, and celebrated life's ups and downs with me. I'll miss him.

"Everly, let's go." Henry's hand lands on my back, herding me toward the waiting car. "Say goodbye to your friend."

"I love you so much. Thank you for everything." I give Christian's hand one final squeeze.

"I love you too. Stay strong. Be fierce. Remember who you are." Our fingers slip apart as the distance between us widens. He blows a kiss, forcing a smile I'm sure he doesn't mean. "And if that hunky prince doesn't treat you right, he'll have to answer to me." He shouts down the sidewalk, oblivious to the disapproving frown of Henry's bodyguard. "I'll go Brooklyn on his ass. I mean it."

Through a watery haze, I smile back at him. Emptiness spreads through my chest, eroding the tattered shreds of my heart, leaving an empty cavern in its place. This is it. It's done and over and I'm lost.

"Is the jet ready?" Henry speaks over his shoulder to Shasta, his assistant. Black sunglasses shield his eyes. Power and confidence ooze from every inch of his body. A passing woman gives him a double-take through the screen of his bodyguards, but he doesn't notice.

Too late, lady. He's mine. Despite my misgivings and heartache, I can't help a burst of pride. The most eligible bachelor in the world just left the market for me. Me. Everly McElroy. Feeling better, I wave at Christian before he disappears into a separate car. In a few minutes, he'll be on his way back to New York City, my hometown, to resume a life I no longer belong to.

"Yes." Shasta is breathless from keeping pace at Henry's side. "Ready and waiting, Your Royal Highness."

"Great. We've wasted enough bloody time today." Without a backward glance, he disappears through the open limousine door. I follow him into the cool darkness and settle onto the seat across from him, confused by the abrupt shift in his mood. Yesterday, he'd been kind and concerned, a rock amid chaos. Today, I don't recognize him. It's like someone flipped a switch and left me with a cold, heartless man. Is this what I have to look forward to?

Once the car is in motion, he removes his sunglasses and

focuses his intense gaze on me. Shasta and his other minions follow in separate vehicles, leaving us alone. Slickness gathers between my legs at the fire in his gaze. The sexual tension between us, a combination of lust and animal attraction, never recedes. I don't know much about him. I'm not even sure I like him, but I can't stop thinking about how he's going to feel inside me on our wedding night.

"Come here." With two fingers, he motions for me to join him on his side of the car. My heart pounds furiously against my ribs. He pats the supple leather upholstery beside his thigh. "Don't get shy on me now, Everly."

"I'm not." No one has ever accused me of being shy. By nature, I'm outgoing, outspoken, and assertive. However, I'm not myself right now. Maybe it's because my father, the former Vice President of the United States, has ordered a hit on my life. Or perhaps it's because Prince Heinrich's tall frame overpowers the spacious interior of the limo. His knees are spread wide, claiming dominance over the backseat. He rests his hands, palms down, on the tops of his thighs and waits for me to obey his command. I slide to his side of the car, leaving a foot of space between us.

"Closer." His baritone carries just enough grit to suggest he's not a man to be trifled with. I edge closer until my knee brushes his trousers. A shiver of need shimmies up my leg. Chemistry isn't going to be a problem for us.

"Are you afraid of me, Everly?"

"No." Despite my denial, my voice shakes.

"Good." He captures my chin between his thumb and forefinger, tilting my head to bring my gaze to his. The pad of his thumb brushes over my lower lip. I press my thighs together, squelching the sharp tug of desire. One corner of his mouth curls upward. "We're in this together."

"I know." His reassurance helps loosen the tight knot of anxiety in my gut. If it weren't for this man, I'd be running for my life, always looking over my shoulder, waiting for a bullet or blade or worse. He's saved me from certain death, but have I traded one hell for another?

"This isn't the time to lose your nerve." When his hand drops back to his lap, part of me is disappointed. He drums his fingers in a restless tattoo. "The hard part is over."

"You don't have anything to worry about. I'm ready." Which is a total and complete lie. Mystery shrouds the future. I'm on my way to a foreign country, with a husband I've known less than a collective week, to begin a new life as royalty. I've never been less prepared for anything.

"Look at me." He reclaims my chin, forcing me to look at him. I blink away. His eyes are too bright, blinding in their intensity. "I'm committed to you and this marriage. We will make it work."

Hollow promises mean nothing to me. Past experience has taught me to expect lies and betrayal, the same as every other man in my life. Many failed relationships have hardened my heart. This marriage is nothing more than a business deal. Man, I'm a cold bitch. I muster a smile. "I hope we can at least be friends."

"Oh, we're going to be much more than that." His gaze drops to my mouth and holds there. The ache between my legs grows into a flutter. The setting sun highlights the details of his face; the small scar above his left eyebrow, another one on his upper lip, and the evening stubble sprouting on his jaw.

At the airport, he threads his fingers between mine and leads me across the tarmac to the silver-and-purple private jet. The staff greets us with cheerful congratulations. Inside the plane, sumptuous white leather sofas stretch along the walls lit by soft gold lamps. All the way at the back, a set of double doors opens into the bedroom and a stunning king-sized bed. His gaze follows mine. We buckle into plush bucket seats facing each other. The engines whine as we taxi down the runway.

His gaze follows mine to the bedroom. A smirk twitches his lips as he reads my thoughts. "We'll get to that later."

"Okay." Heat collects in my face. I brush my hair forward to hide my embarrassment.

"Nervous?" Amusement lightens his customary scowl.

"A little." The words stick in my dry throat. I press my sweaty palms together, trying to hide their trembling. Is he going to take me straight to bed, or will he seduce me first? Either way, I'm ready to get it over.

"Don't be." The nose of the jet tilts upward as the wheels leave the ground. He tugs on the knot of his tie and unbuttons his collar, revealing a triangle of tanned skin and curly hair. "As I promised, you don't have to do anything you don't want to."

But I want to. That's the problem. I want to feel the unbearable friction of his hard cock inside me, bringing me to orgasm, and forcing me to feel anything but the misery of the past few days. Sex is a welcome distraction from my problems. And if history is any indicator, he'll pound every single thought from my head.

Henry watches me through hooded eyes. What mysteries lie behind the veil of his thick, dark eyelashes? Once the plane levels off and the captain lifts the seatbelt restriction, my pulse races. This is it. I'm going to fuck this gorgeous prince, my husband, and I'm going to like it. A lot. Again.

Henry stands and extends his hand. "Ready?"

My knees quake as he shuts the doors of the bedroom, separating us from the staff. We've hardly been alone at all since he proposed yesterday. His Manhattan hotel suite had been filled with assistants, advisors, and handlers. The reality of what I've done hits home with equal parts of terror and excitement. Heinrich Von Stratton, Crown Prince of

Androvia, is about to take me into his bed and ravish me. I suppress a nervous chuckle.

He wastes no time stripping out of his shirt. The expanse of his chest is thick with muscle and covered with a sprinkling of hair. A dark trail dips down to his belly then below the waistband of his slacks. His nimble fingers unclasp his belt, slide the leather through the belt loops, then open his fly. I swallow at the massive bulge behind the silk of his boxer briefs. He's already turned on. By the time my eyes return to his face, he's wearing a cocky grin. His pants fall to the floor. He steps out of them and kicks them aside. "Your turn."

Blood rushes through my ears, drowning out the chaotic thudding of my heart. I lift my hair and spin around, exposing the back of my dress to him. "Will you unzip me?"

"With pleasure." The zipper growls and parts. Cool air rushes over my exposed skin. He leans forward, pressing his lips to the curve of my shoulder, sending tingles along my spine. His breath is hot against my back. "I've been waiting for this moment all day, and I'm going to enjoy every minute of it."

I turn around to face him. He's so close, I can see the gold flecks in his blue eyes. The silk dress whispers over my shoulders and puddles at my feet. I lower the straps of the white satin bra, unhook the clasp and toss it onto the floor next to his pants. He steps back. The weight of his gaze crawls over me. The seconds drag by. He takes his time, inspecting every inch of my body, lingering on the tight pink points of my nipples, the small appendix scar above my hipbone, and stopping at the tiny triangle of white lace covering my sex. I resist the urge to cover myself and let him look. After all, this isn't our first time. We've had casual sex twice before. If you can call a mid-day hookup and some light bondage at a voyeuristic club casual. This time, however, this time is different. More meaningful, more intense. When his gaze returns to mine, his eyes are almost black.

"Take your panties off."

Oh, dear lord. I'm ready to combust from the bite of his command. I hook my thumbs into the elastic strings on my hips and lower them, taking my time, teasing him. He studies my bare pussy for a minute then runs his tongue over his bottom lip. I like the feeling in control of his desire, of having the upper hand after being a pawn in everyone else's game. The power is dizzying.

He steps forward, bridging the gap between us. The scent of his cologne is spicy and sharp. "No more shaving this." The heat of his palm cups the space between my legs. "Is your hair red here too?"

"Yes." My throat aches at the gentle glide of his fingers over my inner thighs. The backs of his knuckles brush my sex. I draw in a breath, waiting for the sing of blood to subside in my ears.

"So beautiful." His hands skate along my hips and press against the small of my back. He pulls me against him, flattening my breasts against his hard chest, and drops his lips to my ear. His voice buzzes against my earlobe. "Breathe, Everly. Relax."

The circle of his arms releases the wariness in my muscles. I nuzzle my nose into the crook of his neck, inhaling the masculine fragrance of his skin. In his embrace, I feel protected and safe. And I need it badly—even if it's an illusion. My eyelids drift closed. The length of his cock presses against my belly. He's heat and hardness and strength, a refuge in the shitstorm of my life.

"Don't let go." In a tempest of uncertainty, his large body anchors mine. I need to forget the mistakes I've made, the trusts I've broken. Just for one night.

In direct opposition to my request, he backs up a few paces. My body sways, drawn toward him by an invisible magnetic force. He lifts a hand to prevent me from following him. "Do you have any idea what I'm going to do to you tonight?"

The moisture evaporates from my mouth. After dragging my tongue over the rough surface of my lips, I try to speak. "I can't even guess." The second time we had sex, he'd strapped me to a bench, spanked my ass until it glowed, and fucked me from behind. The memory of it soaks my panties.

"I've thought about it a lot—how I'm going to throw your legs over my shoulders and sink so deep inside you that you scream my name." One of his hands slips into his black boxer briefs to grip his cock. He strokes it—up and down, over and over. The crown peeks above the waistband, eager for freedom. "But before we begin, I need to make a few things clear about what I expect from you."

The authority in his voice dissolves the strength from my knees. In the background, the jet engines hum, echoing the sing of adrenalin through my veins. "You're scaring me."

"Fear can be healthy." He grabs his discarded belt from the corner of the bed, doubles it, and smacks the loop against his palm, like he's testing it. The thwack of leather against skin reverberates through my body. "But fear isn't what I want from you."

"You want to dominate me." Aside from his hand on my bare bottom, no one has ever hit me. It's a few yards from where I stand to the closed bedroom door. Even if I make it there, where will I go? We're cruising above the clouds over the ocean. My pulse escalates until I can hear my heartbeat in my ears. "I'll warn you now. I'm not very good at taking orders."

"You see, what turns me on isn't cable ties or whips or pain." The angles of his face sharpen as he lowers his head toward mine. With the tip of his nose, he traces the curve of my jaw then nuzzles aside my hair. The softness of his lips brushes across the shell of my ear, light enough to send a shiver down my back. His breath heats my earlobe. "What I want is much more precious and infinitely more difficult to acquire. I want to own you. Inside and out."

* * *

PRE-ORDER YOUR COPY of <u>The Rebel Queen</u> today!

ALSO BY JEANA E. MANN

PRE-ORDER TODAY!
THE REBEL QUEEN DUET
The Royal Arrangement
The Rebel Queen

AVAILABLE NOW
The Exiled Prince Trilogy
The Exiled Prince
The Dirty Princess
The War King

Pretty Broken Series
Pretty Broken Girl
Pretty Filthy Lies
Pretty Dirty Secrets
Pretty Wild Thing
Pretty Broken Promises
Pretty Broken Dreams
Pretty Broken Baby
Pretty Broken Hearts
Pretty Broken Bastard

Felony Romance Series
Intoxicated
Unexpected
Vindicated

ABOUT THE AUTHOR

Jeana is a *USA Today* and *Publishers Weekly* bestselling author from Indiana. She gave up a career in the corporate world to write about sexy billionaires and alpha bad boys. With over twenty books, three series, and many awards beneath her belt, she's never regretted her choice to live out her dream. She's a free spirit, a wanderer at heart, and loves animals with a passion. When she's not tripping over random objects, you'll find her walking in the sunshine with her rambunctious dogs and dreaming about true love. Subscribe to Jeana's newsletter and get the inside scoop on new and upcoming releases, giveaways, and much more! CLICK HERE

* * *

TEXT ALERTS -
text the word "Jeana" without quotation marks to 21000 and get new release alerts straight to your phone.

CPSIA information can be obtained
at www.ICGtesting.com
Printed in the USA
FSHW020030020221
78249FS